Creed

VLG – Book Eight

Vampires, Lycans, Gargoyles

By Laurann Dohner

Creed by Laurann Dohner

Angel was whisked away from a life of abuse as a child when a guardian angel flew her in his arms and gave her to a Lycan couple to raise and love as their own. It was inevitable that she developed feelings for her elusive savior, the GarLycan who protects her pack. As she matured, those feelings deepened to something more after spending time with him, only to be rebuffed by her hero. Dejected, Angel left the pack, moving away to distance herself from the pain. Now, years later, her mother has called her home. Their pack guardian is in need…

Creed is emotionally distant and cold. He's had to become that way to survive his harsh life. His one weakness is Angel. She deserves a happy life, something that he can't give her. He was born into servitude and isn't allowed to take a mate. But, every thirty years he goes into one night of heat. The ravage is upon him, and Angel is determined to be there for him. He'll take her to his lair, chain her down, and finally be able to touch her…

Creed and Angel soon discover their one night of bliss has dangerous consequences.

VLG Series List

Drantos

Kraven

Lorn

Veso

Lavos

Wen

Aveoth

Creed

Creed by Laurann Dohner

Copyright © August 2017

Editor: Kelli Collins

Cover Art: Dar Albert

ISBN: 978-1-944526-87-0

Creed - VLG – Book Eight

By Laurann Dohner

Prologue

Rage burned inside Creed as the drunk woman chased the child too close to the burning fire pit. The girl appeared about five years old, and terrified. She tripped, barely avoiding falling into the flames. The woman leaned down, grabbed her hair, and viciously yanked her up, forcing her to stand. The sound of her striking the child with her hand was loud even from fifty yards away. He winced.

"Do you see what I have to put up with? You're not even mine," the woman yelled. "That son of a bitch you call daddy went into town drinking and whoring again, leaving me to take care of your worthless ass. I should drown you in the river and do myself a favor. That bitch who birthed you had the right idea when she took off and left you both."

Creed dropped down from the low branch and stalked closer to the decrepit cabin. The stench of piled-up garbage, wood rot, and an outhouse couldn't even be diminished by the sooty smell of burning logs inside the fire pit.

The woman shook the child, and then threw her on the ground. She wasn't done. She kicked the little girl as she attempted to get up and run away again, sending her rolling in the dirt. "That's exactly what I should do. It's not as if that piece of shit gives a damn about you either. You're useless. You're nothing but a whiney little brat and I—"

Creed walked up behind her, swung out his arm, and the back of his hand struck the woman hard enough to send her flying. It wasn't a killing blow but he knew she'd be hurt.

She hit the ground and stayed there, unmoving, but he picked up the sound of her breathing.

He crouched down, staring into tear-filled blue eyes. The little girl had bruises already marring the pale skin of her face and one glance down her body revealed more on her too-thin arms and legs. Her tears had left tracks through the layer of dirt covering her cheeks. He studied her hair. It was a ratted blonde mess that probably hadn't been brushed or washed in at least a week.

"Hello." He softened his usually brusque tone.

Her little lips quivered but she didn't say a word. She just peered at him with a look of resigned terror that made him wish he'd hit the woman harder.

"I'm Creed. What's your name?"

She didn't move, reminding him of a frightened deer trapped by a predator. He didn't blame her for being afraid of him. He kept still, giving her a chance to adjust to his presence.

"I'm not going to hurt you. Do you know what a guardian angel is?"

She gave a slight nod of her head.

"That's what I am tonight." He let his gaze wander over the yard. Two broken-down vehicles rusted away next to the cabin. The roof sagged and the porch had only one remaining post, the others already on the ground. Vegetation had grown over them, revealing they'd been in that sad shape

7

for a long time. The adults had just tossed trash bags out the door until a pile had grown eight feet high and almost the length of the side of the cabin. The outhouse didn't even have a door.

He tried to hide his anger. He wouldn't allow a dog to live in those kinds of deplorable conditions. His attention fixed on the little girl.

"Do you live here with just her and your daddy?"

She nodded again, moving more of her head. Some of her fear had eased.

He forced a smile. "Do you have any other family?"

"My mommy went away. I don't remember her. I was a baby."

She had missing teeth, and he smelled blood when she spoke. The woman who had struck her had probably caused damage inside her cheek. Her sweet little voice and her words made his chest hurt. Her mother had abandoned her to a father who left her with an unfit drunk. Children should be protected, not neglected and abused.

"Does your daddy hit you?"

She lowered her gaze and moved her arms, hugging her waist.

Creed clenched his teeth, wishing the father were there to hit too. He knew the answer by the way she responded. Both adults were pieces of shit. He hid his emotions and kept his tone soft. "What's your name?"

She looked up at him. "Anna."

"How would you like a mother and father who love you? They'd never hit you or make you live like this."

Uncertainty crossed her features. He knew it wasn't fair to place that kind of burden on a child, but he still felt the need to ask.

8

She said nothing.

He made the decision for her.

"Is there anything here that you want? A favorite stuffed animal?"

"I have my pink blankie on my bed."

"Stay still. I'll be right back."

He rose up but moved slow so he wouldn't spook the child. The woman remained on the ground where she'd landed. She was breathing but unconscious. He didn't give a damn if she died.

He entered the house and had to hold his breath. It stank of unwashed bodies, dirty dishes, rotting food. And he quickly found out why the stench of mold filled the area—the roof leaked. The floors weren't even fit to walk on.

He found where the child slept. It was just a large pillow with her pink blanket, which had faded sheep all over it. They made her sleep in a corner of the kitchen, next to an overflowing trashcan and a hole the size of a man's boot where the floor had rotted through. He growled low and fisted the blanket, storming out of the house. He masked his features when he reached Anna. He crouched down and offered it to her.

"This one?"

She timidly took it, as if she were afraid he'd hit her. She had reason for that fear; he glanced down at her body again. She only wore a dirty and worn thin nightgown with short sleeves. Most of her skin he could see held bruises from past attacks. She cradled the blanket to her chest as if it were a shield.

"I'm going to take you someplace where it's happy and good. I know a couple who wants a child more than anything. They will love you." He reached out with slow movements to avoid frightening her but she didn't flinch away when he gently lifted her into his arms. "I'm going to make you two promises you can count on. One is that you'll never live like this again. The second one is that you're going to have a loving set of parents who will make sure you are safe and happy."

He could feel every one of her fragile bones and her lack of weight was alarming. It meant they probably didn't feed the girl often. He rose up, holding her in the cradle of his arms.

"Do you know what guardian angels can do?"

She tipped up her chin, her blue eyes wary but the tears gone. "What?"

"We can fly." He walked away from the fire and the hellish home she'd known. "Have you ever wanted to soar into the sky? It's safe with me. I won't let you fall."

"I don't have wings."

"I do." He adjusted her a little in his arms, wrapping some of the sorry excuse for a blanket around her thin limbs to keep her warm. "Do you want to see them?"

She nodded.

He stepped into a clearing. It was a full moon, so he figured she would be able to watch. He closed his eyes to focus, allowing his wings to ease out. He didn't want to alarm her, so he spread them wide, taking his time. Creed opened his eyes, watching her expression.

She grinned, showing off the lack of her two front teeth, and her blue eyes lit up with joy.

"You're a bird man!"

She looked like a dirty little cherub with that smile and the life that flared in her eyes. "And you're an angel in disguise. That's what I'm going to call you from now on. Okay?"

She nodded.

"Put your arms around my neck and hold on tight. We're going to fly, Angel."

She wrapped her arms around his neck, the weakness in them making him hold on to her a little tighter as he took a few steps and leapt, flapping his wings. They flew above the treetops. He just hoped she didn't become terrified.

Her laughter was a welcome surprise. It was also a sweet sound.

"We're flying!"

"We are." He increased the pace. He'd ventured far from his post that night, needing to visit his clan for a meeting. It was just by chance that he'd spotted that fire and seen what was happening to the child. "It's fun, isn't it?"

"Yes!" Pure joy radiated in her voice.

He pulled her a little closer against his chest. He just didn't breathe through his nose. She needed a bath and clean clothes. He hadn't seen running water in the home, either, which meant they probably only had the river to use. He felt no regret over taking the child. He'd have rescued an abused animal from that dire situation.

It took nearly an hour for him to spot the lights of the village. It wasn't so late that everyone had gone to bed. He knew the child had drifted off to sleep a few times but she stirred when he landed next to the fire pit where the elders sat talking. They all grew quiet, staring at him in surprise. The cause was probably what Creed held in his arms, rather than him being in their midst. That wasn't uncommon.

"Get Rava and Undo," he demanded.

One of the elders rose from his chair and nodded, hurrying off toward one of the cabins nestled nearby. Alpha Picoz came out of the darkness a few minutes later, a grim expression on his face.

"Creed, what's going on?" He glanced at the child, then back at him. "Who is she? Where does she come from?"

Footsteps sounded and Creed turned his head. Rava and Undo wore robes, their feet bare, and looked as if they'd been roused from bed. He ignored the alpha, turning toward them. They stopped a few feet away, both of them looking confused and a bit alarmed. Rava's attention fixed on the child.

"I brought you a gift. I know you weren't able to have a baby."

He saw worry in Rava's eyes, and then a flare of hope when his words and their meaning must have sunk in. He decided he'd made the right decision.

"Rava, Undo, this little girl is named Angel. She needs good parents. I promised her you would give her love and keep her safe."

Rava's mouth parted and tears filled her eyes. She took a shaky step forward, her arms raising to take the child.

Her mate gripped her shoulder, halting her. He frowned.

"It's okay," Creed assured him. "She comes from a bad place. Do you understand? You will when you get a better look at her. You're saving her life."

Rava broke free of her mate's hold when Undo eased his grip. She opened her arms and Creed placed the child in them.

Angel turned her head, a frantic look in her eyes as she met Creed's.

He reached out and touched her dirty cheek with a gentle finger. "This is your new mother and father. They will never hit you or threaten to drown you in the river." He said those words for everyone present, as much as for her. "What did I promise you? Do you remember?"

She nodded.

"I always keep my promises. They will love you and keep you safe. You will have a happy life with them."

He turned around to glare at the alpha of the pack. "She's under my protection now. She stays." It was an order that brooked no argument. The pack *would* accept the human child.

He leapt and flew straight up, knowing the girl was in a better place. He might get into a little trouble when he made his report to Kelzeb. Lord Aveoth would be notified, but he'd take whatever punishment he may face. It wouldn't be severe. It was rare that he broke rules by interfering in the lives of others. But those tear-filled blue eyes had somehow left a mark inside him. He'd felt something for once. It might have been pity but it meant he was alive. He normally didn't care about much.

He returned to his lair across the river from the village and landed on the cliff ledge. Silence greeted him as he entered the cave he lived in.

A part of him wished someone had saved him as a child from the fate he'd been handed. He sighed, stripping out of his clothing to take a shower. "Wishing is for fools."

Chapter One

Twenty-four years later

Angel parked the rental SUV next to her parents' home and turned off the engine. It had been only four months since her last visit but she still wished she could see them more often. It was tough finding work in the middle of Nowhere, Alaska, so she'd moved to Washington state. She'd already used up her two weeks of annual vacation, but she'd gotten an unexpected call that had sent her rushing home.

She removed the keys from the ignition and slid out the driver's side door. Her gaze instantly turned toward the cliff that overlooked their valley.

Was he up there watching her?

She glanced at her watch, seeing the time. It was just past noon. She'd managed to snag an early flight, catch a bush plane, and the drive was only three hours from the small airport. He was probably still sleeping, since he kept guard at night.

The front door of the cabin opened and a grin split Angel's face. "Mom!"

The woman with waist-length black hair ran down the steps and grinned back, her arms opening. They hugged. "My baby."

Angel closed her eyes and held on tight. "What's wrong? I got here as fast as possible. Is Dad okay?"

"Yes. He's great. He's out hunting with the men. I told you we were fine on the phone." Her mom eased her hold around her middle and leaned back, still smiling. "Thank you for dropping everything."

"You called and said it was important. My boss isn't happy but he'll survive. I put in enough overtime to deserve an emergency family visit. I told him I had an uncle who died. And I reminded him that I have a bunch of unused sick days."

Her mother shook her head but looked amused. "Lies are bad."

"So is getting fired. You have to play their games when one is in the human world."

"I wish you lived closer."

"Me too but I love my job. The winters are way better there than here. That's an upside. So what's wrong?" She glanced around. "Where is everyone?"

"The younger ones are hunting and the older ones are all at Joe's, enjoying his air conditioning and satellite television. I think they are watching some kind of sports game."

That amused Angel. She forgot how out of touch with the world everyone in the village could be. "A sports game? Any hint of what kind?"

"Who cares?" Her mother reached up and touched her hair. "When did you stop dying it black?"

She'd been so worried when she'd gotten that call that she'd forgotten. "Um..."

"It's beautiful blonde. I'm not complaining. It's just that you've kept it black since you came to us."

Angel decided to be honest. She hated to lie to her mom. "I only darken it when I come home. The rest of the year, I let it be natural."

"Why?"

"Um..."

Her mother arched her eyebrows.

"I know we had to dye it when I was a kid so no one became suspicious of a blonde little girl living here with black-haired parents. But I got tired of keeping it up and decided to just let it be. I didn't want to hurt you or Dad's feelings, so I use temporary coloring that lasts a few weeks before I visit every summer."

Sadness crept into her mother's features, and Angel wanted to kick her own ass.

"I'm sorry, Mom. I would have dyed it but I forgot. You called and I literally shoved stuff into a pack and drove to the airport so I'd be on standby for the first flight this way. What's going on?"

Rava held out her hand. "It's fine. Come inside. Your father can bring in your bag when he gets back. I'd like to speak to you before he does. This is woman talk."

"Oh no." She clasped her mom's hand but it was with dread. "I know I'm turning thirty at the end of the year, or at least what we think I should turn thirty, but please don't tell me you want to set me up with more men to see if I'll hit it off with one of them. I'm happy being single. I have the worst luck with men. Besides that, I tried the whole date-a-Werewolf-from-one-of-the-packs, and it didn't work out. Remember? I'm human, and they don't let me forget it."

Her mother chuckled, opening the door and leading her into the kitchen. "Sit. I'll get you milk and cookies."

"Shit." Angel collapsed into a chair. "That's bad. You always go for the cookies and milk when you want to share upsetting news. Don't tell me you and Dad listened to the elders and arranged for me to mate a stranger from some pack in Washington. I won't do it. I heard it from them before I left, and they say the same thing every time I visit. But it's outdated thinking when they claim it's wrong to be without a mate and children after the age of twenty-five. Modern times and all that."

Her mother placed two glasses of milk and a plate of chocolate chip cookies fresh from the oven on the table. She took a seat across from her. "We'd never do that. We love you and want you to be with someone you can be happy with. We realized long ago that you probably wouldn't settle down with a nice Lycan."

Angel picked up a cookie and took a bite. She'd missed them. "Yum."

It gained her a smile. "I know they're your favorite."

"So what's up? Cut to the chase." An inkling of fear rose. "Is this about Anna? Did someone come searching for me?" She barely remembered her life before she'd been brought to the pack. The few memories she had weren't good ones. Her biological father had been a mean drunk, and his girlfriend made him seem like a sweetheart in comparison. She had taken to living with Werewolves relatively easily at that age. The pack had accepted and loved her. She'd never stop being grateful to them and her parents. They'd given her a wonderful life. "Nobody has ever searched before. They either didn't care when I disappeared or were relieved. Hell, they probably thought they killed me so they never reported it to the state troopers."

Anger tightened Rava's features. "I wish I knew where they were. I would have killed *them*." Tears filled her eyes. "You were half-starved and covered head to foot in bruises. Bugs had feasted on your little legs and they were infected from the bites."

Angel reached across the table and gripped her hand. "You saved me. I love you so much. You and Dad are the best."

"You were and are our greatest gift. We wanted you so much."

Angel blinked back tears. "Stop or we're both going to end up bawling. It will upset Dad when he walks in."

"You're right."

"So, what's going on and why am I here if it's not that?"

Her mother bit her lip. "Did I ever tell you how wild I was before your father came into my life?"

"You're a Werewolf. No need to explain. All those crazy hormones and no mate. You had game going on with some hot guys."

Rava laughed. "Lycan. You've spent too much time in the human world, but yes, I did have game, as you call it."

"Uh-oh. Did some old lover show up and you need me to help you talk Dad out of killing him because he still has the growls for you? Is this Were trying to lure you away from your mate? Is he that stupid?"

"No." She laughed. "That's not it. I just wanted to remind you that I did have a life before your father. I was twenty-one when I met him. I knew he was the one the moment I saw him. It's what happened when I was nineteen that we need to discuss."

"Okay. You have me very curious," Angel admitted.

"We've had a guardian for a long time. It wasn't always Creed."

The mention of his name made her heart beat faster. "I know the story. The pack made a deal with his people a long time ago. They guard our valley to keep everyone safe at night from Vampires or other things that might want to do this pack harm, and in exchange, any of the unmated women will consider traveling to where they live to meet some of their single men to possibly take them as a mate." Her stomach clenched. "No. I'm not going there to meet guys."

"It's not that."

Angel blew out a relieved breath. "Good."

"This is about me right now, and my past. The guardian before Creed was named Monolith. He was this gorgeous hunk of man. He had silver-blond hair and these startling blue eyes."

Angel grinned. "You did him?"

Her mother blushed.

It was something she had never seen before and it made her laugh. "You went to bed with a GarLycan? Wait. Was he a half-breed Lycan and Gargoyle or was he a full-on Gargoyle? I know some members of that clan aren't mixed-bloods."

"He was a half-breed, and don't look so amused. I was curious and young. Back then, we had a lot more women than men in our pack. It's why I had such a difficult time finding a mate. All the good ones were

20

taken right off the bat and what was left wasn't so great. The older girls would tease the strong, good-looking younger men before they were even at the age of consent, so when they reached it, they already knew who to claim. I didn't stand a chance until your father visited our pack. He was looking for a new home. I found my mate."

"You once thought about mating with a GarLycan?"

Her mother hesitated. "It's not that simple. You know how we go into heat?"

"You went into heat so you decided to jump on this Monolith?"

"No. GarLycans don't suffer from heat but they do have this thing called the ravage."

Angel laughed. "Wow. He ravaged you?"

"Be serious. This is important."

"Okay." She sobered.

"It happens every thirty years for them. It lasts one night. You know they aren't the most feeling or emotional beings."

Pain sliced through Angel. She knew that all too well. "I do. Stone cold is their motto, or so it seems."

"Exactly. For one night, they lose all control. They're emotional, and I don't know how to explain it except it's their version of going into heat. It's some kind of instinctual or hormonal thing that happens to make certain their race survives. Like we go into heat so we're assured that we birth children. Monolith knew the ravage was coming on, and he asked the single women in our pack to volunteer to spend that night with him. I put my name in and he chose me."

21

Angel studied her mom. Lycans aged slowly. Her mother didn't look a day over twenty-six, even though she was actually fifty-five. "Of course he did. You're beautiful, Mom."

"Thank you. They have this ritual they do. I was so nervous about that, but I was the adventurous type. He wasn't looking for a mate. He just needed someone to be there for him."

"You mean he needed someone to have sex with."

Her mother nodded.

"What kind of ritual? I'm curious."

"They ask for single women to volunteer, then the guardian will choose which one he wants. The evening of the ravage, he'll ready his bedroom to receive her and she will prepare her body."

"Okay. Weird."

"She removes all her body hair from the neck down and soaks in a bath so only her natural scents remain without artificial ones. They don't like any chemical smells." Her mother glanced at her hair and bit her lip. "Then they tie the woman down on their bed. It's to prevent her from getting hurt."

"He tied you down? Kinky, Mom."

"It was for my safety. Monolith explained it to me beforehand. He knew he'd lose control, and that I didn't want him for a mate. He wasn't looking for one, either. They tend to avoid it for as long as possible. It's a weakness or something to them, when they mate. You know how solitary they are."

Boy, do I. Bitterness still left a bad taste in Angel's mouth, remembering her teens and right before she'd moved away. She just nodded.

"They don't get totally naked. He had me wear this thin gown. Think like a towel wrapped around your body that hooks together under your left arm. It falls from breast to mid-thigh. He wore one around his waist. They just move them out of the way where necessary. It's to avoid as much skin contact as possible so they don't get the urge to claim a woman as a mate."

"It sounds cold."

Her mother blushed again. "Not exactly."

Angel arched her eyebrows. "Do you want to expand on that?"

Her mother glanced out the door, then lowered her voice when she looked back at Angel. "He had me drink some of his hormones first."

"What?" That stunned her. "You had to bite him?"

"No. It's complicated but it's just a little drink, and it kind of put me into heat, only more intense than that. It's what they do."

"Don't tell me you had to give him a blow job or something. I don't want to hear that. You're my mom."

Rava laughed. "No. I probably would have if he'd asked, but I was tied down for that very purpose. No touching him. It helps them not mate a woman during the ravage."

"You had to kiss him?"

She turned her head and pointed at the base of her skull. "They get this bump right here. It fills with their hormones. Don't tell anyone. He

23

swore me to secrecy but I was as curious as you are. I didn't want to drink just anything he gave me. They use a needle to withdraw it. It's how they know the ravage is coming on. It starts to build up there and they can feel it. Anyway." Her mother paused. "It was amazing. I've had great sex before, but he was *very* memorable. I couldn't even talk for a day afterward. I was hoarse from screaming."

"T.M.I, Mom."

"Your clit swells up and throbs. You hurt from wanting sex. He touched me and I came. Then he entered me and we went at it for hours. Lycan men are excellent lovers, but a GarLycan during the ravage is far more intense. I lost track of how many times he made me c—"

"Okay. Enough. Got it. Get to the point—besides shocking me with your past sexual exploits."

Her mother bit her lip again. "Yesterday, Creed showed up and spoke to the elders. The ravage is upon him. He asked for volunteers. It's tomorrow night."

Angel forgot how to breathe for a few seconds. Pain squeezed her chest. "You brought me here for *that*? So I could know which woman he chooses?"

She stood so fast she almost knocked over her chair.

"You know he rejected me when I practically threw myself at him. I..." She blinked back tears. "I was in love with him. I don't *want* to know. Why did you call me here?"

Her mother stood and rounded the table. She wrapped her hands around her upper arms and locked gazes with Angel. "I called you because no one volunteered. He's not as social as Monolith was when he was our

24

guardian. Creed rarely speaks to anyone except the elders and our alpha. The women are afraid of him, and there aren't many single women who haven't taken mates."

Angel let that sink in, and more pain flooded her. "So you called me because you think I still want him? Even for a night? I practically begged him to give us a chance. Then he flew away every time I even approached him after that. He'd stay up on his cliff and not come down. No thanks. He'd reject me even if I offered. I'm human. He went to the elders asking for a Lycan woman, didn't he?"

Her mother tightened her hold. "Yes, he did. I've never lied to you. I won't start now. I know he hurt you. You always had the biggest crush on him. He brought you here and rescued you from your before life. You almost had hero worship. I know it pained you so much when you told him how you felt and he stopped talking to you."

"He broke my heart." Angel blinked back more tears.

Her mother nodded. "I know."

"Then why did you call me?"

"Monolith shared something else with me when I was with him for the ravage. Creed could die if he goes through it alone." Her mother spoke quickly. "I debated on calling you or not. In the end, I didn't think you'd ever forgive me if he died and I didn't give you the opportunity to save him."

The information stunned her.

Her mother nodded. "Imagine being cold inside for thirty years, and then all of a sudden having all those emotions overwhelming you at once. That's what happens to them. They don't know how to handle it. The ravage can make them insane if they don't have someone to focus it on. Monolith told me some just attack the walls and become self-destructive. Others do worse. He lost his brother that way. He flew into the air as high as he could and then allowed himself to plummet to his death. They injure themselves so badly that they can't heal fast enough. He said it's rare but it happens. I'm not saying Creed will face that horrible fate, but he is at risk."

Angel closed her eyes.

"I wanted you to have the choice, baby."

Angel nodded. "He won't agree to it though." She looked at her mom. "I'm human."

"You might be all he has. He needs you now, Angel."

"I have to think about this."

Her mom released her. "I understand."

Chapter Two

Angel fled out the back door and glanced at the cliffs. She knew approximately where Creed's home lay. She'd spied on him as a teen until she'd spotted where his lair had to be located. It was impossible to reach unless he flew someone there. She'd never been invited. At one time, she'd wanted him to take her to his home more than anything.

She made a beeline for the river, where memories lingered of the days Creed had spent time with her when she'd been a teen.

She reached the rock that stretched out over the rushing water and climbed out to the edge. She took a seat and allowed her legs to dangle. A memory surfaced of Creed sitting next to her, holding a fishing pole. They'd talked for hours. She even knew a bit about his upbringing. His parents had four children, so he'd been sent away from home. It was a GarLycan thing, something to do with too many males living in close proximity. They were territorial and tended to fight. His clan leader had assigned him to be their guardian. It was far from their territory and gaining access to Lycan women as potential mates for their clan was a priority. GarLycans birthed more males than females on average, which left them always in need of women.

Most of the pack didn't think Creed had a heart. She knew that was false. He'd saved a lonely, terrified little girl once and flown her to a wonderful life. He could have just ignored what he'd seen but he hadn't. It proved he possessed compassion and he'd cared about her. He'd even given her a new name.

Years had passed when they hadn't spoken after that night he'd given her to new parents, but he'd become her companion when Lycans her age were out hunting and learning their senses in wolf form during their teens. She'd been left to her own devices. He'd probably felt sorry for her, but she liked to think they'd been soul mates, that he'd been lonely too.

Angel had made the mistake of telling him she was in love with him when she'd hit the age of consent. She had hoped he'd admit he felt the same. She'd dreamed of Creed flying her up to his lair and mating her. Her gaze lifted and she zeroed in on the location of his home. The opening wasn't visible but she thought she had identified the boulder it hid behind. All her hopes and dreams had rested up there with him.

He'd crushed them by telling her that loving him was a mistake.

He'd given no real explanation or apologies. He'd just flown away and avoided her. She'd spent a week in bed, crying her eyes out, and then had tried to get his attention to talk to him again. He either ignored her or just refused to come down. Either way, as the months passed, she'd decided to leave her home and start a life somewhere else. She refused to continue to stare at those cliffs, seeking any sign of him. It was painful to always catch herself looking up at night, into the sky, hoping to see him flying above her.

Loving Creed had changed her life in so many ways. He'd given her a home and then taken it away. She'd wanted to return to live in the village after a few years but the career she'd started only allowed her those two-week visits. Every time she came to visit her parents, it brought back the pain. No man could ever compare to Creed. She'd made some horrific mistakes trying to get over him.

Tomas's face flashed in her mind as she peered into the river. He was a Lycan she'd dated. He'd been good looking and was seeking a mate. She'd given him her virginity since Creed hadn't wanted it. Their relationship had seemed happy for the weeks it had lasted, and she'd wanted to love him. She had even talked herself into believing she did, out of desperation—until she'd brought up the future and kids. Tomas had informed her she was good enough to date and sleep with, but he wanted a Lycan mate when he settled down. She'd ended the relationship and he'd let her go without a protest.

She'd dated Mitch when she'd first moved to Washington. He was human and a fun-loving guy. They had grown serious and had even talked about marriage. Again, she'd wanted to love him. She'd tried. It had almost been a relief when she'd come home early after a small fire had shut down the building she worked in, and she'd caught him in bed with some woman. She'd packed her stuff and left. He'd tried to talk her into coming back but she was done. She hadn't even cried.

Then there had been Adam two years before. He'd been her neighbor. They'd started out as friends, then became more. It had come as a shock when she'd realized he was doing drugs. The signs had been there but she'd been naive.

The confrontation was bad when she'd told him to stop or they were over. He'd tried to get physical. That had been a mistake. She'd been raised with Lycans. Her parents and pack mates had taught her how to fight. He might have thrown the first punch but he's the one who had been taken away in an ambulance. She'd moved to a new apartment.

Her experiences with previous relationships sucked because she was in love with Creed. None of them had ever stood a chance of making her forget him. But he was the very definition of emotionally unavailable.

She lifted her gaze to the cliffs. Creed was the toughest man she'd ever met. Was it possible this ravage thing could take his life? She hugged her chest and fought tears. She'd always wanted him, but would one night ever be enough? And how bad would it be for her to live with afterward, knowing what she was missing?

She had no answers.

Movement from the corner of her eye drew her attention and she turned her head. Four large wolves crept out of the woods. She smiled.

"Hi, guys. I'm home."

One of them rushed forward and jumped up on the rock. She reached out and scratched Amond's coat on the back of his neck. He flashed teeth at her and bumped his head against her shoulder. She laughed.

"It's good to see you too. No clothes nearby?"

He shook his head and licked her cheek. She pushed him away. "Gross. I don't know where that tongue has been." She leaned back, staring at the smaller version of him. "Tell your brother how wrong that is."

Tonni growled. Her tail wagged and she turned toward the village. Amond backed away but he lightly gripped Angel's wrist with his teeth and tugged.

"Okay. I'll see you guys in about ten minutes. Go put some clothes on. My mom made chocolate chip cookies. We'll meet up there."

Amond released her wrist and lifted a paw, batting at her hair.

She glanced at it. "What do you think? You didn't recognize me from behind, did you? The wind is blowing in the wrong direction for you to pick up my scent. Did you think I was an intruder?"

He whined.

She gripped his muzzle and pushed. "What were you going to do? Bite me? I know what a sweetheart you are. You probably would have let me rub your belly if I were a stranger, like some playful puppy. Go on. I'll see you in ten."

They ran off and she sighed. They'd want to know why her hair wasn't black anymore, and why she'd returned when they weren't expecting her. She needed to think up something to tell her friends. Her gaze lifted to the cliffs and she tensed.

A dark figure loomed in the sky—and it soared right at her.

Creed's wings were tucked and he plummeted fast. He almost hit the river before he braked the descent by opening his wings. She felt fear for a second at the sheer speed with which he could move, and the fact that it seemed as if he were going to slam right into her. She actually leaned back, expecting the impact, but his wings opened wide. One powerful flap had him jerking to a halt. He landed on the rock a foot away.

"Who the hell are— Angel!"

He was still as gorgeous as ever. His jet-black hair fell to his shoulders. It was silky to the touch and baby soft. She remembered that. His eyes were a stormy dark blue. It was the swirls of silver that gave them that appearance, like lightning flashes in a midnight sky. Long, thick black eyelashes accented them. She'd always envied him those. His full lips pressed together, giving him a harsh expression. It didn't detract from his looks at all. Nobody did brooding better than Creed. He was sexy regardless.

She glanced at his body as he tucked his wings behind his broad shoulders. It was a shame, because he had lovely black ones. They weren't feathers, but some type of soft texture that came from his Gargoyle blood. He'd allowed her to touch them a few times and it had reminded Angel of velvet.

"Hello, Creed." She finally got her voice to work, refusing to drool over his muscular arms revealed in the thin-strapped black tank top he wore. She knew he liked them because they didn't rip when he sprouted his wings.

"Your hair. I'd forgotten it used to be blonde."

"It's still blonde. I just didn't hide it with dye this time."

He looked angry when his eyes narrowed. "What are you doing home? This isn't your time."

She stood. Her legs felt shaky and she hated how short she was compared to him when they were close together, but he was a freaky height of six feet five. Any woman would feel that way unless she was over six feet tall. She brushed off the ass of her jeans.

32

"My time? Am I not allowed to come home to visit my parents when I feel like it?" She knew she was trying to pick a fight but old heartache wasn't easy to get past.

"Of course." He took a step back. "I saw you interact with the wolves and thought you were a lost hiker. They didn't transform."

"Amond is a little too old to flash his goods at me. I'm grateful for that. We're not kids anymore. I'm sure he's grown a bit since then. They might be comfortable with the naked thing but they know I'm not, since I don't have a reason to strip in front of them." She paused. "Is that how you deal with strangers? Swoop down at them like an angry demon and give them heart attacks?"

He scowled. "No. I capture them and go retrieve a VampLycan to wipe their minds of anything they've seen, before I send them on their way."

"That's good to know. You're still keeping the pack safe. I thought you were only on duty at night."

He glanced away. "I was awake."

She glanced at her watch. "You're up early."

He looked back at her then. "Is everything okay with you?"

"It's all great," she lied. "Why do you ask? Is everything okay with you?"

"You only come in early summer."

He ignored her question. She didn't blame him. It wasn't as if he'd confess the ravage was about to hit him. That would mean he might actually ask her to help him out. She studied his eyes, really looking at him.

There was a tiredness to them that hadn't been there before. It concerned her, then irritated her. He'd shut her down when she'd admitted to caring about him. It was a mistake to show him she still did, and that wasn't something she was willing to do. He'd probably just fly off.

"Well, I'm not some nosey hiker trespassing on pack land. I was just visiting my old fishing spot."

"I remember. We spent a lot of time here."

It stunned her that he'd mention that. "That was a long time ago."

His gaze locked with hers. "Yes, it was."

"I should go. My friends are meeting me at the house. They've had enough time to put on some clothes."

She spun away, making it a few feet before he spoke.

"You look good, Angel."

She halted. Her heart raced and faced him again. A wariness settled in. He was probably just being polite by giving her a compliment...but Creed wasn't one to do that. He usually didn't say anything unless there was a reason. She stepped closer and tilted her head, studying him.

"What?" His body tensed.

She walked up to him until they almost touched, really gazing into his eyes. They were bloodshot on closer inspection, and he actually looked a little pale. The guy always had a deep tan, even in winter. She reached out and placed her hand on his bare skin just above the material of his tank top. Alarm hit.

"You're cold."

He jerked away but couldn't go far on the rock without falling into the river. "I'm a GarLycan."

"You usually run hot unless you're shifted." She reached up and pressed her hand against his neck. "You're cold to the touch, Creed."

"I'm fine."

She didn't believe him. "You're lying."

He growled.

She took a step back, stunned. That was new. She didn't even know he did that. Emotion flashed in his eyes for a split second before he masked it. That was also unlike him. Sure, he could laugh when amused and show anger, but that looked as if it were an unintentional slip.

Her mother's words replayed through her mind. Was he already losing control? Were his hormones playing hell with him?

She reached up again and drew so close, she almost pressed against his body. She ran her fingers through his hair and he closed his eyes. He even tilted his head a little to allow it, almost encouraged it.

She stroked his hair and moved her hand, running it up the back of his neck. There was a large lump there at the base of his skull. He groaned when she brushed over it and actually wavered a little on his feet. Angel was mesmerized.

Creed gripped her hip with one of his hands. "Stop."

She ran her fingers over the lump again, gently caressing. He actually leaned into her, pressing his chest against hers as his eyes closed once more. His mouth parted and he groaned deeper, a sexy sound. He even pushed the front of his jeans against her belly. The feel of his stiff cock surprised her. Creed was turned on.

"Look at me," she whispered.

He opened his eyes to reveal the color of them had turned more silver. "Stop, Angel. Please." He put a few inches between their bodies.

"Or what?" She didn't want to let him go. Creed finally wanted her. It was a powerful, wonderful thing to have him at her mercy. She'd been at his before, and she didn't want to walk away, the way he had. His head fell forward, and she would be able to kiss him if she just lifted up on her tiptoes. The desire to know the feel of his lips against her own tormented her.

A muscle in his jaw clenched and his fangs slid out. "Don't play with fire."

She placed her other hand on his side. "You already burned me, Creed."

He appeared confused. "I don't..."

"Don't what? Understand? Want me?" She slid her hand over his stomach and lower, down to his hip. He shivered, his body quaking from the light touch. She dared to explore the front of his pants with her fingertips. "Is that a cell phone in your pocket or are you happy to see me? Let's find out."

He grabbed her wrist and jerked it away from the front of his pants. "Stop. You don't know what you're doing."

She still had her other hand on the back of his neck. She caressed the bulge there again, letting her fingers play over it. Creed's gaze dropped to her lips and he growled deep. His hold on her wrist and her hip tightened until it almost hurt. She did stop caressing him before he broke something on her without meaning to. She hadn't been raised around non-humans without learning the dangers of their strength.

She made a decision. "I know exactly what I'm doing."

"You don't."

She cupped the base of his neck so he couldn't jerk away and rose up on her tiptoes. She didn't go for his lips, but instead pressed her cheek against his and whispered in his ear. "I'm going to volunteer to get you through the ravage."

He released her wrist and grabbed her other hip. He shoved her back a few inches and snarled. She had to lower to her feet but didn't let go of him, so he couldn't get too far away. Pure rage twisted his features and those fangs were close enough that she got a really good look at them.

"No."

That hurt. "Why not? Because I'm human?"

"No."

"You just said I look good. You're as hard as a rock." She looked down at the front of his jeans. The outline of his cock was clear and impressive. "Not a cell phone." She glared up at him. "You're not flying away this time. No hiding. So tell me. What is it about me that you detest so much?"

His coloring turned a little gray. "It's not that. Is that what you think?"

"I threw myself at you and practically begged you to take me to your bed before I moved away. Am I ugly to you? Repulsive? Do you hate me because I'm human? What is it about me that makes you always reject me?"

"You deserve better. I can't give you the emotions you need."

She stared up at him. Was he trying to protect her? She'd never suspected that.

"You deserve more," he rasped, drastically lowering his tone. "I could never make you happy. I'd rather not have you at all than watch you slowly die the way my mother did."

"Your mother died? When?"

"Eleven years ago. She was a full-blooded Lycan." He closed his eyes. "My father is a full-blooded Gargoyle. He couldn't give her enough affection to sustain her. She slowly lost the will to live. That's what women do when they have their hearts broken repeatedly by their mates. I take more after him."

She had to lean forward to catch his words. "I'm so sorry." She hurt for Creed. She knew he had a close connection to his mother. Her death must have happened around the same time that she'd thrown herself at him. It was all making sense...and it was devastating.

He turned his head away, closing his eyes. "Don't volunteer, Angel. Not you. You're more than just a vessel to be used by me for a night. I'd never forgive myself, and I don't think I'm sane enough right now to pick someone else. I'm supposed to protect you, even if that means from myself. Let go of me. I need to get far away from you."

She did the opposite instead, and went up on her tiptoes again. She threw her other arm around his neck and pushed against his chest until their bodies were flush together. "Listen to me, Creed."

He wrapped his arms around her waist and held her. She noticed the lack of warmth coming from his body even more, and it scared her.

"What?"

"It's my choice, and I want to be there for you. I know it's only a onetime thing. You want to avoid hurting me? Don't make me lie awake tomorrow night, knowing you're with someone else. You were there for me when I needed you the most. Let me be there for you."

He lowered his head and bent his knees a little, burying his face in the crook of her neck. "I don't want to hurt you."

"Then come get me tomorrow night. Do you need me now? Let's go."

He held on to her a little tighter. "It's going to hit full force tomorrow night."

"What about tonight?"

"You wouldn't survive two nights of me like this."

"I'd be willing to risk it."

He rubbed his face against her hair and throat. "Let go. I'll meet you here at six tomorrow evening. There are things you need to do. I told the elders."

"The ritual. I know. I'll do it. Are you going to be okay? You can take me home with you now if you want."

"Angel," he growled.

"I'm right here."

"Let go. Tomorrow."

"I'll buy a damn grenade launcher and blow you out of that cliff if you don't come get me. Am I clear?"

He barked out a harsh laugh. "Yes."

"I mean it."

"I know you do."

She eased her hold on him and the second she did, he jerked away and dove off the rocks. His wings spread out before he hit the water, and then he was shooting into the sky. He flew away up to his cliff as if the hounds of hell were after him. She watched until he was back inside his lair. That wasn't like him either. He never returned there in broad daylight, when anyone could watch to see exactly where he landed.

She bit her lip, really worried. He'd hurt her in the past but she still loved him. She probably always would.

"I'm going to be there for you," she murmured.

Chapter Three

Angel frowned at her mom. "Is Dad still sulking?"

"I think so. He's upset. You're his baby girl."

"Lycan girls go have sex with men. That's acceptable but this isn't? Can you say double standard? I'm almost thirty."

Her mom grinned. "That's what I told him. You're totally my daughter. He worries about you."

"Because I'm human."

"Yes. We always worry about you. You aren't as hardy as Lycans."

"Thanks." She wasn't offended.

Her mother chuckled. "I know it's not fair but it's true."

"I know. I get colder easier since I don't grow fur." She lifted her hands out of the water in the tub. "No claws to tear into frisky boys. I swear I thought Dad was going to kill half the males in our pack when I hit sixteen and some of them came sniffing after me."

"It was a real concern. They are horny, persistent things at that age, and you couldn't exactly defend yourself as well as the other girls. When I was that age, I batted a lot of them around when they became too fresh."

"I bet your parents didn't try to stop you when you *did* decide to have sex. It's Lycan nature. You go through heat."

"That's true. I guess we got spoiled since you didn't suffer from that. Your father warned all the boys that you were fragile and reminded them that you could get pregnant."

41

"I don't have that freaky thing where I have to have a pep talk with my body so my ovaries start producing eggs like crazy. Mine do that every month on their own."

"Exactly. Speaking of..." Her mother hesitated.

"I'm on the shot. I have been for at least seven years."

"Okay. That will work with Lycans but I'm not so sure about GarLycans. It wasn't a problem for me. I knew I wouldn't ovulate. You're different."

"Humans can get knocked up easier."

"Yes. And don't forget that if you consume blood from a Lycan, it can mess with human contraception. Let's just assume it's the same way with GarLycans."

"You said I'm going to have to drink his hormones. Not his blood."

"True."

"I'll be fine."

"Your father is just worried. You bruise so easily, and you've only slept with one Lycan. He was really careful with you by following all the rules we set forth for him to touch you. Your father made sure of it."

"Oh my God." Angel shot her mother a horrified look. "Are you kidding me?"

"Sorry, baby. We wanted to make sure you didn't get hurt. Lycan sex can be pretty rough. Your father explained the differences to him. That was all."

"Great. I'm glad I didn't know that at the time. I would have been so embarrassed."

"We're always looking out for you. It's time to get out."

Angel eased out of the tub and looked down. "Did I get it all?"

"I don't see any hair on you. I wonder if Gargoyle women are hairless. It's kind of odd, isn't it? Especially since they mate with Lycans. I've always wanted to ask one of the mates if they have to keep all the hair off until they shift."

Angel used a towel and dried off, before letting her hair out of its clip. She'd washed it earlier, wanting it to be dry by the time Creed arrived. "I could ask him tonight."

"He's not going to be in a mood to talk." Her mom lowered her voice. "Monolith barely said ten words to me the night he took me, besides telling me what to do. They don't seem to be able to think straight."

"Oh."

Worry creased her mother's brow. "Are you sure about this? It's very rough sex. They lose control."

"I'm sure. Creed isn't going to hurt me."

"You just don't heal as fast as we do."

"I'll be fine." She hung the towel and picked up the almost sheer material that someone decided to call a dress. "This is it?"

"Yes. I told you. They avoid skin contact but it's almost as if you're wearing nothing. Just wrap it around you, under your arms, and I'll secure it for you."

"Thanks for helping me."

"I bet your human friends don't discuss these things with their mothers or help out this way."

Angel laughed. "Um, no. They don't."

"Humans are too uptight. Sex is a natural, healthy thing."

"Lycans don't get STD's, Mom. Humans do. They can also get pregnant by jerks who don't stick around. There aren't enforcers who track down and severely punish their men who hit women. A rapist Lycan would be a dead one. The entire pack would track and kill him. Your world is a lot safer than theirs is, in that regard."

"That's true."

She walked over to a mirror. "How do I look?"

"Beautiful."

"You'd say that if I were dipped in mud." Angel smiled to soften the words.

"Smartass. Should I mention that it's not your face he'll mostly be staring at tonight? Are you going to be okay with being tied down? I felt a little panic at first. It's unnatural to do that to our kind but I just breathed through it when he put on the restraints."

"It's not my first time. I'm not some blushing virgin."

"Humans are really into tying each other up?"

"Some are. I'll be fine. I don't want you sulking too."

"I'll keep your father occupied. Don't give us another thought. This is your night."

Angel took a deep breath and blew it out. "I've always wanted Creed. I'm just nervous."

"Once you drink his hormones, thinking and worrying won't be a problem. That is some powerful stuff. I was really surprised because

44

they're so cold, but not when the ravage hits. Maybe you shouldn't drink all of it. I don't know how a human will handle it."

"Some Gargoyles in Europe still breed with humans."

"They do?"

"Yes. Creed told me that once. Don't worry, Mom."

"I won't. I want you to have fun and enjoy finally being with Creed." Her mom hugged her. "Now it's time to go so you aren't late. Sneak out the back door. The elders are on the prowl. You know how they like to put their nose in our business. They think Creed is going to pick you up at the front door, and I didn't correct them."

"Thanks. I just hope I don't run into anyone. Good thing it's still warm out. Imagine having to wear this in winter." She looked down at the thin dress. "This thing would also get me arrested in Seattle if I stepped out in it. Indecent exposure. You'd have to send me bail money."

"I'm going to go to your father. He's pacing and growling. I hear him."

"Shit."

"I can handle his mood, and it's not as though he can go after you."

"True. Not without some serious climbing gear."

"Go. Creed might show up early."

Angel exited the bathroom and raced down the hallway to avoid her father. He was protective, and she didn't blame him. It just proved his love. She eased open the back door and glanced around. There was no one within sight, so she took off. The path through the woods wasn't occupied and she made it to the meeting spot quickly. She stared up at the cliff. Her heart hammered. Excitement and nervousness battled for dominance.

"Come on, Creed. Here I am. Come get me."

He won't back out, will he? No. He needs me. He said he'd be here and he always keeps his word. She bit her lip, staring at the cliff face. She didn't see him. It was possible she was a few minutes early or he was running late.

A twig snapped behind her and she spun.

Creed stood there, and she relaxed. He'd come for her. It just wasn't by air. He must have gotten there before she had and just stayed out of view.

His eyes were mostly silver as he strode forward. He wore a black cloak with black pants. Both were new and kind of attractive, if unexpected; different from his usual jeans and casual wear. His feet were bare. He didn't speak, but instead just walked right up to her.

She gasped when he scooped her up into his arms, and then his wings expanded, the cloak folding between them along his back, out of the way. He leapt and she wrapped her arms around his neck. He flew toward the cliff.

Angel turned her head, watching them glide over the river. Faint memories returned of when he'd first found her and taken her to a new life. It was the only time he'd ever taken her into the air. She'd asked when they used to hang out but he'd always refused. It seemed appropriate that they were flying together now. She smiled, loving the sensation of soaring high. She wasn't afraid. Creed wouldn't let her fall. His arms were firmly hooked under the back of her knees and her waist.

He did a sharp movement when they reached his ledge that jerked them to a stop, and he just dropped straight down about five feet. He cushioned her landing in his arms. The mouth of the cave was bigger than she imagined it would be. He strode inside and she peered around with open curiosity. She'd always wondered what his lair was like. He'd dodged any and all questions she'd ever asked about it.

Lights were on deep inside, once they'd made a few turns. The fact that he had electricity came as a surprise. The tunnel ended with an open doorway. She glanced at the thick metal and wood barrier. He paused long enough to use his foot to slam it closed. He walked forward through a living area. It contained a small kitchen that had a fridge, microwave, and propane cooktop. It was basic but effective. There was a television and couch.

He carried her through another short tunnel and into a lit room. The bedroom was small, and the bed took up most of it. She gaped a little at the king-size four-poster frame. It was the last thing she figured he slept on.

Creed stopped at the end of the bed and gently lowered her to her feet. She noticed the chains laying on the thick black comforter. They made her swallow hard and face him. His eyes swirled with colors and movement, seeming alive.

"Hi."

He frowned. "Are you sure, Angel? There's no turning back after I share my hormones. Yes or no."

Her mother had said he probably wouldn't be in a mood to talk. "I'm sure." She looked down and noticed more chains near the end of the four-poster. She stepped over to the foot of the bed. "Do you want me on it?"

He spun away and walked to the small dresser. There was a shot glass sitting on it, filled with clear liquid. He picked it up and hesitated.

She didn't. She held out her hand. "Give it to me."

"Drink half. I'll give you more if you need it. I don't want to overdose you."

"Is that possible?"

"Your heart could give out." He looked grim.

"Half it is."

He closed the distance and held out the small glass. She hoped it wouldn't taste bad. It wasn't blood. That had to be a bonus. She dropped her gaze from his and just lifted the thing. *Half.* It couldn't be any worse than downing a shot of tequila. She drank.

She'd expected it to be bitter but was surprised by the sweetness. She stopped drinking and looked at what was left. She'd judged it right.

He took the glass and returned it to the dresser. The cloak he wore reminded her of something out of a Vampire movie but she didn't say anything. It could be part of his ritual. He returned to her and pointed at the foot of the bed. "Turn around and bend over."

She hadn't expected that. The mattress was high, but she did as instructed. His tone was a little harsh, his eyes swirling silver and blue. He reached over and grabbed one of the chains. He pulled it, and that's when she saw the leather restraints at the ends of them. His hands shook as he

48

gently took one of her wrists, belting it so only soft leather touched her skin. He tightened it, but not so much that it cut off the circulation to her fingers.

A hot flash suddenly hit. She'd never had one before, but knew what it was when heat seemed to spread throughout her body. It was uncomfortable but she tried to relax. She was bent over the bed though, on her tiptoes to be able to get her hips high enough to rest on the mattress. Creed restrained her other wrist so they were spread straight out to her sides. She tested them when he backed off her. She had a few inches of movement but not much more.

She looked over her shoulder and watched him crouch behind her. His fingers wrapped around one of her ankles. "Relax," he demanded.

He pulled her foot to the side and it left her standing on one leg. He belted that ankle and she understood what he was doing. It would leave her unable to stand when he restrained the other and would keep her legs spread apart. She lowered her head, closing her eyes.

Another blast of heat coursed through her body and she breathed through it. Creed had secured one ankle and took the other. With her upper half lying on the bed, she wasn't in danger of falling. He secured her other ankle. She wiggled her toes. She couldn't feel the floor or anything else within reach of her feet.

Her nipples beaded tight and her clit started to throb. It was his hormones. Her mother said it was like going into heat for Lycans, only stronger. She'd always wondered what that experience would be like. Every second that passed made her more aware of her body. Her skin felt super sensitive and her pussy began to ache.

"You're okay," Creed assured her. His voice grew even deeper, taking on an inhuman quality. "Just breathe, Angel."

"Why chain me down?"

"So you don't fight me. I can't hurt you this way."

Clothing rustled and she turned her head, forcing her eyes open. Creed stepped into her view. He'd ditched the cloak and his bare chest glistened in the lights from a fine sheen of sweat. He was breathing a bit heavy, too. She lifted up a little more to take in the view of his abs. He had a very fit body, every muscle defined. He'd removed the pants and now wore the same material as her dress, wrapped around his hips like some thin towel, open on one side where it split. She got to glimpse his hipbone and leg but nothing more.

He stepped behind her and his hands brushed against the back of her thighs.

Angel moaned at the slight touch. It felt extraordinary and only made her ache more. "Creed."

"You're almost ready."

Almost? She wanted him. Her pussy was wet. She could feel that, and her clit throbbed, ached. Her stomach quivered and her breasts almost hurt from how tight her nipples had become. The heat flowing through her body had her breaking out into a sweat, too.

He shifted the material lying over her bent body to expose her backside and it tickled a little. His hands returned but now nothing was between them. He had roughly textured fingertips and they caressed the back of her thighs, slowly trailing upward toward her ass. She tried to shift closer but couldn't with the way he'd restrained her.

50

She cried out when he suddenly slid one of his hands between her thighs and cupped her sex. His thumb brushed across her clit and he rubbed. She knew she was soaking wet because he spread it across that bundle of nerves.

"I want to fuck you," he snarled.

"Do it," she urged.

She clawed his bedspread with her fingers. It was a thick, soft material. The mattress heavily padded. None of the wood from his bed touched her. He drew a circle around her clit and she moaned louder, almost ready to come just from those few movements.

"So beautiful."

She barely understood his words. Blood rushed to her ears and she tensed, trying to buck against his hand. He needed to rub her just a little more. She'd come. She was on the edge. He shifted his hand and ran his thumb over her clit again. She sucked in air and moaned. One of his fingers teased over the slit of her pussy and she arched her back.

"Creed!"

He slid a thick digit inside her pussy and rubbed her clit with his thumb. The sensation of any part of him inside her was enough to send her into climax. It was brutal as it ripped through her. Her nipples tightened even more, painfully so. She cried out.

"Son of a bitch." Creed jerked his finger free, and then he pressed something thicker and larger against her pussy. The crown of his cock rubbed down her slit then hovered right against that opening. He pressed in and gripped her hips with both hands in a near bruising hold.

He entered her in one long, slow thrust. He was big, but it felt so good that Angel yelled his name. He snarled and drove into her deeper. She clawed the bed, still coming down from the climax. He almost totally withdrew from her body but then surged forward, filling her. Angel cried out as pure ecstasy shot through her. She squeezed her eyes closed and her heart felt as if it were going to explode inside her chest. It was too much sensory overload, but Creed withdrew and thrust again. He moved faster, fucking her harder.

There was only Creed, the feel of him fucking her, driving her beyond her limit of pleasure. She fought the restraints, wanting to touch him. They held her securely, her legs spread open for him, and she cried out when the second climax struck.

Creed released her hips and came down on top of her. His weight pinned her to the bed as he drove in and out of her with a fury of passion. His hands slid up her sides and he reached under her chest to cup her breasts in his hands. He squeezed, giving her nipples a slight pinch between his fingers. Angel cried out as she came a third time.

She moaned and tried to buck him off. It was too much. It felt too good. No one could survive what he was doing to her. But she couldn't move away. He pounded into her harder, more snarls coming from his throat. He caressed her breasts again, massaging them. Angel opened her mouth, biting the bedspread as she moaned. She came again. Her vaginal muscles convulsed hard, squeezing around this cock.

Creed buried his face against her back, his hot mouth kissing her shoulder. "Angel," he moaned. "My Angel."

She came yet again. He teased her breasts with his fingers, his cock driving in and out of her so fast, she felt as if they were going to ignite in flames. His cock seemed to get even harder, if that was possible, and then he twisted his face away, roaring out. The sound almost hurt her ears but it didn't matter. She was gripped in another white-hot haze of pure rapture.

Creed stilled on top of her. He panted and she could barely catch her breath. Their heavy breathing filled the room. He lifted some of his weight off her back and rubbed his cheek against her shoulder blade.

"Are you okay?"

"Yes."

The heat burned her up. The need. She wiggled her ass, arching her back. "More."

He moved slowly, almost totally withdrawing from her, and then drove in deep. Angel murmured his name. He turned his head and she felt his fangs brush against her skin.

"Fuck. No!" He jerked his mouth away from her.

"Yes! Don't stop."

"I want to bite."

"Do it. It all feels so good."

He snarled and began to fuck her hard. The bed banged against the rock wall near the headboard and the wood frame seemed in danger of breaking. It didn't matter. She clawed the bedspread and fought the restraints. She just wanted to touch him, but her arms were spread out to her sides and she couldn't even reach where his hands still gripped her breasts. He squeezed them and she came again. It almost drove her out of her mind. She lost the ability to think. There was just Creed's cock moving inside her, his weight pinning her down, and his hands on her breasts.

Creed came so hard it damn near made him pass out. Angel was so hot, wet, and tight that she was killing him. He understood why his kind hated the ravage so much. It was the most painful, yet exhilarating thing they could feel. He was an animal at that moment, pounding his dick into the woman under him. And he loved it. He loved *her*.

Angel cried out his name and he clenched his teeth together. The slight taste of blood was on his mouth. He'd nicked his lower lip with his fangs just to keep from sinking them into Angel. He wanted to bite into her and taste her blood. He wanted to possess every part of her. The claiming need was upon him. He'd known to expect it. He'd survived the ravage once before but it had never been so strong. It was almost too overwhelming to resist.

He tried to force himself to straighten up, to get off her. That's why they restrained women. It gave him the ability to fuck her without going near the woman's throat or shoulders. She wasn't just any woman under him, though. It was Angel. He'd shoved the dress she wore out of the way so his skin was plastered against hers. He loved the way she felt. So soft, slick, and warm.

Her scent filled his nose. He opened his eyes, staring at her creamy skin. Those bare shoulders of hers taunted him. She tossed her head, almost catching him in the chin. He looked away, watching her fingers dig into the bedspread. He wanted to feel her fingernails tear into his skin instead. He came just thinking about how it would feel. He roared her name. She moaned his, and her pussy convulsed around his dick.

He closed his eyes, riding through his seed filling her. A new desire arose. He wanted her with his child. He started to move again, even though it almost hurt from how good it felt. Images of Angel pregnant, her belly swollen with his son, flashed through his thoughts. He even formed a picture of what it would look like with her holding his child in her arms.

He wanted it so bad. His dick hardened until he actually had to glance at his arm to make certain he wasn't transforming into his other form. His skin wasn't gray. Paler than normal but still all flesh. He pumped his hips harder, faster, driving them both into another shouting match when the passion broke. He stilled, panting.

Angel's ragged breathing alarmed him. She was human. He worried about her. "Angel?"

"Mind blown." Her voice was a mere whisper. "Good thing."

It was too much for her. *He* was too much for her. He released her breasts and she whimpered. He felt like a bastard as he lifted off her back and stood. He gently withdrew his dick. He was still hard, his dick aching. He didn't smell or see blood. He relaxed a little. She was so small. Fragile. He stared at her ass. She had a wonderful one. He didn't like women too skinny, and his Angel had curves. He opened his hands and couldn't resist palming her cheeks.

"Don't stop. I need you," she pleaded.

She arched her back, lifting her ass into his hands. He eased forward a little and didn't even have to guide his dick. He was too hard to need to.

He just pressed against her pussy and slid home. He threw back his head as she took him and her moans were all the encouragement he needed. He let go of her ass and reached out, grabbing the posts of the bed with both hands. He let nature take over, fucking her until his knees wanted to give out and he was snarling her name as he came hard.

Chapter Four

Angel knew she'd survived when she woke. Every muscle seemed to ache. The heavy weight on her back and the warm breath that fanned her neck made her smile though. Creed had made it through the ravage, and she felt it was appropriately named. She muffled a laugh. He'd ravaged *her*. She tried to shove her hair out of her face, but chains rattled and her arm wouldn't bend more than a few inches.

She was still restrained. The last thing she remembered before passing out was Creed giving her water to drink and gently cleaning her. He'd also adjusted the chains at the side of the bed, moving them to the top so she could lie more on the mattress instead of just being bent over it. Her ankles and legs had been freed. He'd collapsing on top of her after that and brushed kisses along her shoulder. The heat faded to a warm glow inside her body. The need for Creed to fuck her had calmed. He'd come down from the high of his hormones soon after she had. Not that she'd had any complaints.

"Creed?" Her voice came out raspy, her throat dry.

He tensed over her and his breathing changed.

"Can you untie me yet? I need your bathroom."

"Yes." His voice sounded gruff.

She stifled a laugh. He was probably experiencing the same issues as her. She just hoped he ached a little bit less. He slowly moved off her and unbuckled one wrist. She bent that arm, stretching it up. He undid her left arm last and she rolled over.

Creed stood at the end of the bed with his back to her. "I'm sorry I fell asleep. But you did, and I just thought I'd let you sleep for a little bit before I took you home."

She sat up and adjusted the so-called dress. He had on his towel garment but it was a bit askew. She grinned at the line of beefy ass that showed. She noticed his coloring then. He was a golden brown again. He looked healthy and sexy.

"It's okay. Do you know what time it is?"

He crossed the room, not looking at her. He opened a drawer and peered inside. "Damn."

"What?"

"It's past noon. We slept the morning away."

She eased off the bed and cringed when she stood. Her legs were wobbly but held her weight. "I didn't have anywhere to be. Did you?"

"No."

"Where's your bathroom?"

He pointed to the closed door in the corner. "There."

"May I use it?"

"Of course."

He wouldn't look at her. That hurt. She hadn't ever had a one-night stand before but she wasn't liking the aftermath of her first experience at all. He could at least act as if she were a person. Instead, she felt as if he wanted her gone. Pain came first but it was quickly followed by anger. She walked past him and opened the door. She didn't glance his way. Two could play that messed-up game.

The bathroom was a surprise. She expected a compost toilet in his cave but there was actual plumbing. It was a little crude in the rock-hewn room, but still nice. She closed the door and shook her head. GarLycans were pretty ingenious with making their cave dwellings comfortable. She quickly used his flush toilet and decided to shower while she was in there. The shower was a lower section of the room, with a drain in the floor and a hanging hose-like faucet. It would probably make him pricklier that she planned to get clean before he took her home, but she didn't care.

The water wasn't hot but comfortably warm. She sniffed his shampoo and liked the scent. She took her time, and then dried off, putting the dress back on since it was all she had to wear. She borrowed his toothpaste and used her finger to clean her teeth. She opened the bathroom door finally and found him sitting on the end of the bed. He met her gaze. His eyes had returned to their normal stormy blue. He also looked as if he'd showered. She wasn't certain how that was possible, but his hair was freshly wet.

"Two bathrooms?"

"I have an outdoor shower above. I climbed up there since you were taking your sweet time."

"Why do you have a second one?"

"I don't think you want the answer to that."

"I wouldn't have asked otherwise."

He hesitated for long seconds. "So I don't have to clean up inside if I come home bloody. I can wash outside."

She wasn't shocked. GarLycans and Lycans sometimes dealt with violence. It was just a fact. Creed's job was to protect the pack, and she

59

was sure blood had been spilled on many occasions over the years. "That's smart. I'm ready to go."

He arched an eyebrow.

"What? You want me gone. Let's go."

"I didn't say that."

"You wouldn't even look at me. I got the message loud and clear."

He stood. "It's because I feel guilty. I was trying to think of a way to apologize. I'm sorry."

"I knew what I was getting into."

He narrowed his eyes. "Really? Because I didn't mean to keep you chained down and pass out on top of you. That came as a surprise to *me*."

Angel shrugged. "We were both pretty worn out."

He came closer. "How are you feeling?"

"The shower helped. How do you get warm water down here?"

He hesitated. "Do you really want to know?"

"I asked. It's pretty clever."

"I installed solar panels for electricity and keep water tanks above. They refill when it rains. They're metal and they heat up in the summer. I also have a propane water heater for the winters. It doesn't get as hot as your homes would but it's more comfortable than trying to heat water and take a bath in a plastic tub."

"And the toilet?"

"I drilled in water and waste lines. That wall isn't too far from the edge of the cliff and a small ledge. It and the sink aren't hooked to the hot water but come directly from the collection containers above that store

60

all the rain water. That's what I use for the kitchen too. I boil anything before I use it for cooking."

She glanced around the bedroom. "How did you get that big bed in here?"

He grinned. "I had my brothers help. We flew it in pieces and put it together. I helped them with their homes too."

"It's very comfortable and big."

He came even closer. "Was it everything you thought it would be?"

"You have a nice home."

He reached out and fingered a long wet strand of her hair. "I meant what happened between us."

She stared into his eyes. They made her feel a little weak in the knees when he looked at her like that. She swore it was passion she saw but dismissed it as hopeful thinking. He was over the ravaging. She debated on lying. She decided not to answer at all.

His features tightened. "Did I hurt you?"

"No."

"Would you do it with me again in thirty years?"

He wasn't going to let it go. Maybe he needed to ease his conscience or was looking for a compliment. "In thirty years, I'll be almost sixty. I doubt you'll want me by then. I'm human, remember? Those aren't Lycan years."

His hands clenched at his sides. "Isn't your mother sharing her blood with you to slow your aging?"

"No."

He turned a little ashen. "I thought she'd started doing that when you turned twenty-five. We discussed it and that was the plan."

"You discussed that with my parents? Why?"

He said nothing. Which irritated her, but she figured he had brought her to the Lycans when she was a child, so it shouldn't come as a surprise that he might want to know about her life. It actually made sense once she thought about it.

It was also a little nice that he kept tabs on her. It softened her anger.

"Plans change. I left here to live in the human world. I'd need to take blood from her on a regular basis to do it. That's kind of hard since they don't like to leave the pack and I only get two weeks of vacation time every year. It could also trigger me to change into a Lycan at some point. I wasn't willing to take the risk."

"You'll live longer."

"And I could die. It happens sometimes. Long-term blood taking when it's not from a mate can trigger a violent change without warning that few survive, or worse. I could start rejecting the blood, and it would shut down my internal organs one by one. I'd rather live a normal human lifespan than risk two out of the four possible outcomes if I accept the blood. My chances aren't good at fifty-fifty."

"Two out of four?"

"Sudden violent shift that's usually fatal; rejection of the blood resulting in death; I change over without it killing me; or nothing goes wrong, and I just slow down in aging."

"I didn't know that."

"Now you do."

"Why does being a mate matter?"

"He'd be drinking my blood as well, and it would change his chemistry to be more in line with mine when I take his. Every pregnancy would help too. It would change me enough gradually while I carried his offspring, making for an easier transition if his blood were to turn me into a Lycan. The rejection rate is extremely rare that way."

"You should take your mother's blood. You're a part of the pack. You're not considered human and shouldn't have to die the way they do." His tone changed, anger coming through. "I'll discuss it with your parents again."

"Don't bother. I made up my mind. I'll live a normal human lifespan."

"I won't allow you to die of old age!"

She managed to keep her mouth from falling open over his angry outburst. She grew suspicious though. It wasn't like him to lose his cool. Not Creed. He was usually indifferent. "The only other option is allowing my parents to arrange for me to mate some strange Lycan, and hope he'd treat me as good as if I were a Lycan." She was testing his response.

He snarled, his fangs sliding down. His eye color changed. The blue turned so dark it appeared black, the silver glints startling, like torn pieces of light coming through a pool of utter black.

Angel reached up and gripped the back of his neck. He didn't flinch away but he did stiffen. She felt the base of his skull. The lump was smaller but she still felt it. He lifted his hand and wrapping his fingers over hers.

"What are you doing?"

"You're still emotional."

He growled. "I'm not emotional."

"You are." She used her other hand and placed it on his chest. He was warmer than he had been the evening before but not hot. "I thought the ravage only lasted one night."

"It's just some remaining hormones that need to work out of my system today. I should take you home."

She licked her lips. "Or we could go back to bed for a few hours."

"I'm too wired to sleep."

"Who said anything about sleeping?"

She twisted her hand under his and it made him lose his grip. She caressed that swollen spot on the back of his neck. He closed his eyes and leaned toward her.

"That's kind of sexy. Most men respond that way when you do this." She let her other hand slide down his chest and over his stomach. He clenched his muscles under her exploring palm. He didn't try to stop her when she hit the material around his waist. She stroked his cock and felt the instant response. He hardened.

"Angel, don't."

"This again? Don't you ever learn? I never listen."

He snapped his eyes open and they were pitch black, all the silver gone. "You should."

She wasn't afraid. His eyes would probably have sent others running for their lives. They were dark and gleaming, a little evil looking. But she didn't believe that about him. It was also a Lycan trait, only he wasn't about to shift into a wolf. "Do you know how irresistible you are when you're like this?"

"Are you angry with me?"

"No." She pressed up against him and wrapped her fingers around his stiff cock, giving it a gentle squeeze. "I just love seeing you a little unleashed."

"Don't push me, Angel. I'm still having control issues."

"Now you're just teasing me."

He grabbed her by her arms, tearing her hands off him. "What are you doing? Are my hormones still in your system?"

"Why? Because I want you. That's nothing new. I don't need to drink anything to feel this way." She slowly pulled out of his hold and opened her hands on his chest. "I just have to look at you, Creed. The next time you need someone like this, I'm going to be some white-haired grandma. You won't want me then."

"No. I'm not going to let that happen to you. You'll take Lycan blood to slow your aging and I'll bring you back here."

"I'll be mated to a Lycan if I'm still young-looking. I think he'd mind you carrying me off. I would too, if he's my mate." She pushed and he stumbled back a few feet. It caught him off guard or she never would have been able to move him. She glanced at the bed and then threw herself at him. They both fell, landing on the mattress.

Angel climbed on top of him and straddled his thighs. She reached up and untied the dress. Creed clenched his teeth but his fangs puffed out his lips a little. She tossed her dress aside and leaned forward, opening her hands on his chest again. She loved the feel of him under her.

His gaze ran over her naked body.

"One more time, Creed. You get to be on bottom this round. I want to ride you." She curled her fingers and lightly raked her nails down his skin and over his abdomen. His muscles rippled and a moan escaped him. She untied the material at his waist and he didn't try to stop her. She parted it, baring his cock.

He was big. She knew that from feeling him inside her. He was hard already, responding to her. "I could look at you all day," she admitted. "Touch you all day."

"You need to get off me. You don't know how dangerous this is."

"You're not going to hurt me." She leaned all the way over and opened her mouth, sticking her tongue out to run the tip of it over his nipple. It puckered instantly. She did it again and then closed her mouth over it to suck. She nipped him gently with her teeth, catching just the tip.

He moaned and his fingers stabbed into her hair, cradling her head there. His cock twitched against her belly. She let one hand trail over the shaft of his cock and dip lower, caressing his balls. He arched his hips under her and spread his thighs to give her freer access. She released his nipple and went for the other one.

"Angel," he groaned.

She sucked on him and stroked her hand back up his shaft. She was getting wet just touching him and hearing the soft rumbling noises that started to come from deep within his chest. She lifted her gaze, watching his face. His eyes were closed, his mouth open to show off those fangs. Pleasure twisted his features.

Creed fisted her hair in his hand but he didn't force her to lift her head away from his skin. She started moving her mouth downward, using her lips, tongue and teeth to lightly bite and lick his ribs, then under them to his stomach. She scooted down his body as she went, until she reached his lower stomach. She lifted up a little and gripped the base of his shaft with her hand. She licked her lips, and then opened up wide to take in his girth.

Creed snarled when she wrapped her mouth around his cock and began to slowly move up and down, using her tongue to rub against the head. He twisted on the bed a little but didn't try to unseat her.

"I'm going to lose it," he warned in a very deep, inhuman voice.

She wanted to smile. Oral sex on men wasn't her favorite but Creed was different. There was something just too sensual about him and his reactions. She wanted him to come. She took more of him inside her mouth.

Creed used his grip on her hair to force her off his cock. She winced a little but before she could protest, he rolled them over. She landed flat on her back and then Creed used his legs to shove hers wider apart. He gripped her knee, lifting it up against his hip. He adjusted and the crown of his cock pressed against the opening of her pussy. He wasn't gentle or slow when he took her.

Angel moaned, loving the feeling of him filling her up. She frantically grabbed the tops of his shoulders and dug her nails in when he started to move. "Yes."

He pinned her knee against his hip with his arm, still holding onto her leg. He fucked her hard, wildly. She hooked her other leg over his waist, digging her heel into his muscular ass. It angled her pussy just right so he hit that spot inside that drove her insane. She rocked her hips, meeting his rapid thrusts.

It felt too good to withstand, and she knew she wasn't going to last after just a few minutes. The climax built, and then she tossed her head forward and tried to muffle yelling his name by pressing her face against the top of his shoulder, next to her hand.

He buried his face in her neck and snarled. A jolt of pain came next but it felt amazing.

She frantically grabbed at his back just to cling to him when the wave of pleasure hit. It wrecked her inside. She felt him come. He shook violently over her and she held on to him tighter. She couldn't think. All she could do was feel. Their bodies locked together while they both rode it through.

Chapter Five

Blood. It tasted so sweet. It filled Creed's mouth and he swallowed. He bit deeper and got more of it. His fangs were locked into Angel. She was holding him but she didn't scream or try to fight him off. She felt so damn good. *Too good. So right*. He swallowed again. His dick flexed and he groaned as more of his semen shot inside her. His entire body tingled and goose bumps ran down his limbs.

His ability to process thought returned—and he realized what he'd done.

His fangs were buried in the crook of Angel's shoulder. It was her blood he'd taken.

He opened his eyes and forced his jaws to part, releasing her. The sight of bright red marring her skin and the drops of her blood on the bedding horrified him.

He lifted his head a little and saw that one of his hands gripped her shoulder, holding her in place. His claws were extended but hadn't pierced her skin. The gray tint to his fingers and the texture change was unmistakable.

He arched away from her more and the side of one of his wings brushed across the bedspread.

He turned his gaze to stare at her face. Her eyes were closed and a little blood reddened her bottom lip and the skin just under it. He twisted his head, staring at where she'd bitten him. Her human teeth had left tiny indents to show where she'd clamped her mouth. It wasn't more than a little welling of blood, but she'd bitten him too. It might have been what triggered him to do the same.

She murmured something and he looked back at her face. Her eyes opened and a small smile curved her lips. "Wow."

He was in shock. That's all she had to say? She wasn't turning deathly white as understanding of what he'd done dawned on her. He expected her to scream or perhaps try to beat at him with her fists in anger. Her smile did fade a little as she studied his face with more alertness. A confused look surfaced, and she let go of his back to touch the side of his face.

"You're partially shelled." She just seemed to accept it when she smiled again and slid her hand back to his ear, playing with his hair with her fingertips. "It's okay."

It wasn't. Nothing would ever be okay again. He flexed his wings hard, the panic that seized him helping. The force of movement when he flapped them sharply jerked him back and off the bed. He hit the low ceiling, pain exploding in the back of his head from the rock. He dropped into a crouch, landing on one knee and bracing his hands as he shook off the pain.

"Creed?"

He looked at her, watching Angel sit up on the bed. She appeared surprised, and then she frowned. She rolled a little, crawling toward the end of the bed.

"Why did you do that? Did you just hit your head? Or were those your wings? I heard that thump." She glanced up at the ceiling he'd slammed into, then down at him.

70

His rage exploded. It was hotter than hell, seeming to ignite his body into literal flames. He felt his skin hardening, cooling despite what was happening inside him. He didn't fight the change. He needed to completely shell his body to keep him locked into place or he might do something catastrophic.

Angel almost fell out of bed as she scrambled toward him. His vision locked on her and everything turned into shades of black and white. She was naked, her beautiful breasts a sight he couldn't unsee, nor the fact that the blood on her shoulder had trailed lower, red, thin rivulets from where he'd bitten her.

She rushed at him and dropped down in front of him on her knees. It probably hurt since he hadn't done much with the flooring besides toss down a thin carpet over the rock. She grabbed his face with both hands, a fearful look in her eyes now. He closed his eyelids at the last second.

"Creed? What's wrong?" Now there was panic in her voice.

He couldn't answer her. The burning inside him hurt. The cool exterior of his body seemed to contain it though. He tried to shut down his emotions. He needed to. Angel could get hurt if he didn't. The walls around them would smash and crack if he threw himself at them now. The entire damn cavern that had been chosen for a guardian to live inside might collapse on top of her.

"Creed? Talk to me. Tell me what to do!"

Her voice had risen and he knew the sound of fear. He didn't blame her one bit. She should be terrified. He shelled his body more firmly, trying to block out the sensation of her touch. It dimmed a little but he remained aware of her hands. He couldn't shut her out. Not now.

He roared in rage inside his head. Pure panic returned. He hadn't reached his hundredth year. He was still obligated to be the guardian of the Lycan pack, or whatever other job he was assigned until he reached that birthday. His father had committed him to servitude, and Lord Aveoth would be ruthless in his punishment. Mistakes were never forgiven.

Grief tore at his heart next. He'd withstand the lashes he'd have to take. Even spending ten years encased in a prison for his crime would seem easy compared to what he knew they'd do to Angel. Death would almost be considered merciful.

No! He'd fall before he allowed her to be taken to the GarLycan cliffs and sentenced with him. They wouldn't have a reason to enslave her if he wasn't there to suffer the knowledge that she was paying for what he'd done. It was the only way to protect her now.

"Damn it, Creed! Please? Just open your eyes and say something. Anything! Did you hurt yourself?"

Her hands explored the back and top of his head, before she moved behind him. She leaned against one of his wings. He hadn't folded them when he'd shelled out his body. They were still extended. She pressed her body along his back, wiggling between his wings to get a better look at the top of his head.

"I don't see any cracks. That's good, right? No dents." She wrapped her arms around his shoulders. He was thicker-bodied when shelled than in skin. She put her lips near his ear. "Creed? I know you're in there. I know you can hear me. You told me that once when I asked if you were aware of your surroundings in Gargoyle form. There's no way you fell

72

asleep that fast." The pleading tone in her voice tugged at him. "Please come back and tell me what's happening to you."

Angel ignored the slight abrasive feel of Creed's rough shell against her bare skin. She'd seen him that way before one other time. She'd thought he was amazing when he'd shown her what he looked like in resting Gargoyle form. Now, not so much. He'd literally used his wings to throw his body off hers from the bed, slammed into the roof, and then hit the floor. His skin had darkened as she watched, turning into that stone quality.

Tears filled her eyes. Had he hurt himself when he'd hit the top of the cave? For all she knew, this is what happened to GarLycans when they died. Maybe their corpses were sold off and people bought the huge Gargoyle statues to put in their yards, never realizing they had once been living, breathing beings. Or perhaps he was just so hurt that he'd blacked out and would remain that way until he came to.

She ignored how he chilled her skin and how uncomfortable it was to hug a big shape seemingly made out of pure stone. It was Creed.

How in the hell had things gone so bad all the sudden? They'd had amazing, mind-blowing sex. Then afterward, when they'd recovered, it had all gone so horribly wrong.

"I'm here," she promised him. "I'm right here. I have you." She looked around his room, searching for any sign of a phone. He might need help, but there was none in sight. He probably had a cell phone. She had left hers at her parents' house inside her backpack. It wasn't as if she'd thought she'd need it when she'd left the house.

73

Where would he keep a phone? She had no idea. She wasn't even sure who to contact. The pack called Creed if they needed help. She didn't even have *his* number. The elders had to have some kind of way to get in touch with his people, unless they always went through Creed. She wasn't sure of how that worked. Only the elders and the alpha knew.

She let him go and almost stumbled into one of his wings. They were big suckers, and she bumped her shoulder on the tip of one as she rushed to his dresser. There were only three drawers. No phone was inside them, but she did find a battery alarm clock. She turned, running out of his room. "Where in the hell did you leave it?"

She couldn't find the cell phone. She opened the two drawers under the counter in the tiny kitchen. It only held utensils and a few other items he used to cook or eat.

"Damn it, where is your cell?"

She rushed into the bedroom, seeing he hadn't changed back. He remained exactly as she'd left him. She darted into the bathroom. There was a cupboard under the sink but it just contained a few spare towels and toilet paper. She returned to his side, shooting a frantic glance around the room. There was no sign of a hamper or any shelf he could have set it on to charge.

Frustration had her considering the odds of going to the entrance of his cavern and trying to wave a towel until hopefully someone from the village spotted her up on the cliff. They wouldn't have any way of reaching her though. Not without calling in search and rescue. No way could humans get involved. They might have helicopters and crews that could reach the ledge where she stood but then what? They'd place her in a straightjacket for seventy-two hours if she led them to Creed and told them he was a real man, not a Gargoyle statue. They couldn't help him anyway.

She got in front of Creed and lowered to her knees. He was beautiful in any form but he took on an ethereal quality when he was all gray and that stone texture. She placed her hands on his shoulders, gripping them.

"Creed? Come back to me. Open your eyes and stop." Her voice broke as she fought down a sob. She'd thought it was bad when he'd flown away and refused to speak to her in the past. This was much worse. "You're scaring me. Do you hear me? Did you hurt yourself so bad that you're in trouble? I can't help you like this. I don't know what to do!"

There was a small cracking noise—and she held her breath. His right shoulder slightly vibrated. She hoped that it wasn't just wishful thinking...but then some of the dark gray of his body started to lighten. She breathed again and watched his face.

"That's it, baby. Come back. Unshell."

The hard mineral under her hands seemed to slightly soften. She squeezed, making certain she wasn't imagining it. It was a relief when she knew she wasn't. Creed moved his head a little but his eyes remained closed. The shelling of his body started to soften more, fading from gray to flesh tone. He parted his lips and sucked air deeply into his lungs. She stared at his chest as it expanded.

"That's it, Creed. Come back to me."

His eyes opened and they were pitch black. She was grateful to see any life in them. The color started to lighten. She felt heat under her hands on his shoulders, as he changed more into firm, supple flesh. It was a slow process but he sagged when it was over. He even withdrew his wings. The little popping sounds she heard as they folded down and withdrew into his back normally would have made her wince but it didn't matter. None of it did. Creed was alive.

She searched his eyes. The blue was back, along with the tiny silver flecks. She leaned in closer, putting her nose so close she almost touched his. "Are you hurt?"

"No." His voice came out too deep, harsh.

"You scared the living shit out of me."

"You should be."

Her mouth parted, and she felt as if he'd emotionally slapped her. Had he done this to her on purpose? She jerked back. "That was cruel, Creed." She released his shoulders. "I thought you might have hurt yourself so bad you were dying." She itched to punch him but fisted her hands instead and shoved them in her lap as she collapsed onto her legs to sit. "How could you do that to me?"

"How could you do this to *us*? Do you know what you've made me do?"

Her mouth hung open. "What?"

"Don't give me that innocent look." Creed rose up and got to his feet. "You got what you wanted, but you have no idea of the cost."

His thunderous voice echoed in the chamber. She gaped at him as he stood before her, looking furious. His eyes silvered out, swirling as if they were liquid metal.

"I told you to stop, Angel. Would you listen? No! You always have to push, don't you? You are so damn human!"

"So you had to get payback by pulling that stunt? I thought you were dying! You're such an asshole."

He threw back his head and roared. Angel cried out from the pain it caused in her ears and covered them with her hands. Dust partials rained down from the ceiling and along the walls, where small cracks in the mountain showed. Her heart hammered as she lowered her hands.

Creed glanced around. "Fuck," he muttered, his voice much softer. "I'm sorry. We can't even have an argument in here. They probably heard that at the village." He glared at her. "This is your fault. Are you happy, baby? Is this all you ever dreamed it would be? Just wait until tonight. That's when the real hell begins."

She stared at him. He wasn't making sense and he was being totally irrational. "You're still emotional and not over the ravage all the way. Take deep breaths. You need to calm down. I'm going to do the same."

His eyes widened, and then he spun away, pacing the room.

She lowered her gaze, hating that she was admiring Creed naked. He did have a nice ass—and every other body part. She was just glad he wasn't gray anymore and he was moving around, even if he did look as if he might wear out the carpet.

He knew every button to push to make her madder than hell, but she tried to remember he was going through the GarLycan version of heat. She could relate to being all over the place with emotions at that time of the month, from having her periods when she'd been younger, before taking a shot to prevent them. He only had to deal with it every thirty years. Men had it easier than women.

He stopped and looked at her. He appeared as if he'd gotten a handle on his anger. "This is what I'm going to do. I'll return you to the village, and then I'll fly to see Lord Aveoth. I'm going to take the blame. I'll tell him I unchained you and provoked what happened between us. I won't let you pay for this, Angel. I would never allow you to be harmed in any way. I'll tell him you're human, and I forced you into this situation. You aren't strong enough to stop me, no one can refute that. You need to say the same thing if the guardian who replaces me ever questions you. Promise me that."

She was confused over everything he'd said but the last part stuck. "You're quitting your job?"

He hesitated. "I'm going to fall, Angel. It's the only way to make certain they can't use you as part of my punishment."

"What punishment? What are you talking about?"

"You didn't know. I understand that. You live by your emotions. It's one of the things I've always found charming and irresistible about you." His features softened. "I want you to know that I will fall with honor to protect you. I wouldn't do it for anyone else."

"Fall? What does that mean?"

"My father swore me to clan service for the first hundred years of my life, to the previous lord. It was done at my birth. I was given no choice in the matter, but I must honor the vow he gave. To do anything else would be dishonorable and not be tolerated."

78

He walked to her and lowered to his knees. He reached out and took her hands in both of his, holding them. "I'm not allowed to take a mate until my service is over. My life isn't my own. I should have told you this. The punishment will be a lashing in front of my clan until I'm required to shell my body. I'll be so weakened by then from blood loss that it's easier to stay in that form for longer periods of time, since we suspend our bodies in that shape. They encase the punished in a sealed cavern for ten years. It won't kill my kind, but there's no sound, not even the brush of a breeze. There's nothing but darkness and being locked with your own thoughts, between sleeps, until the uncasing. It's a very effective way to make certain the laws are followed."

"That's horrible, but—"

"I'm not done," he cut her off. "Lord Aveoth will decide what will happen to the mate. His father swore he'd have them slaughtered. He threatened to make the punished watch. Some lords in the past considered it a mercy if they just enslaved the mate while the punished were encased for those ten years. That way, he wouldn't lose her forever. Remember when I told you that Gargoyles nearly died out as a race because our birthrates for having males is much higher than girl children?"

"Yes but—"

"What is worse than making the punished go into darkness, knowing that his mate will be forced to breed with any single male who wishes to try to impregnate her? Any children born would be taken from her after birth, to be the sole property of the father, her parental rights stripped. It helped keep our race alive, despite the cruelty of it. The mate wasn't given a choice."

His gaze left her to glance at the bed and his mouth pressed into a tight line. "I will never allow them to enslave you. You'd be tied down and taken by any male who was willing to have a youngling with a human vessel. Some of the older full-bloods could use your body to give them sons. They'd keep you locked up until you birthed, take the child away from you forever, then turn you into a vessel for the next one who chooses to make you birth him a child. It would continue until I'm freed. You wouldn't survive it, Angel. Not your body or your mind. And I won't allow that."

She wasn't shocked by the laws he'd just explained. She'd grown up in a Lycan pack. Some of their laws were downright barbaric. "Why would they want to do that to *me*? Why are you telling me this?"

He paled slightly. "You don't know?"

"Know what?"

He closed his eyes and dropped his chin to his chest.

"Know *what*? Creed?"

He looked at her, and she saw a deep sadness in the depth of his gaze. "I lost control. I thought you goaded me into it on purpose by biting me." He held her hands a little tighter. "I changed forms while we were on that bed." He paused. "While I was inside you. I lost control of my forms and I bit you back. I was drinking your blood during sex."

Angel was grateful she was already sitting on her ass. The implications sank in. "Oh God."

He nodded. "We mated. The bond is weak since I only bit you near the end...but it's done."

Chapter Six

Angel refused to believe it. Sure, they'd had sex. He had shifted a little but she was pretty sure it was around the time they'd both gotten off. She could see little marks on his skin from when she'd accidently bit him on his shoulder but they were already healing.

He had bitten her.

She looked at the wound, unaware of it until then. She'd been too freaked out over Creed turning to stone. It ached a little and still bled, but it wasn't life threatening or really painful.

"I don't feel any different. I would. I don't. We didn't mate."

Creed tilted his head, his look unhappy. "We did."

"No. We didn't. It was one little slip at the end. That's all. It doesn't mean we bonded."

"Denial won't help. Believe me. That's why I shelled my skin. I didn't want to accidently hurt you if I began beating on some walls to air out my frustrations. I could have brought the mountain down around us."

"I probably only got a drop or two of your blood. That's not enough. Lycans hav—"

"I'm not just Lycan. We do share our blood with a mate but that's not why. We do it to help her live longer and be stronger. We also give our blood to women when they're carrying our children, so the baby will retain strong Gargoyle traits. I drank your blood while I wasn't in control of my body. That's what mates us. I'm mostly Gargoyle. I told you, I take after my father. I came inside you when I was fluxing and drinking your blood."

"Fluxing?"

"It's what we call between flesh and stone. I looked at my skin. There's no doubt."

"But I barely bit you."

"It's not a matter of sharing blood with a Gargoyle. The second I bit you in that fluxed state, the taste of your blood in my mouth during sex, it triggered hormones to flood my body. Bonding ones. I came inside you while I was fluxing and drinking your blood. It's how we mate." He glanced down at her stomach, then back at her face. He let go of one her hands and reached down between them, resting his palm over her belly button. "I'm inside you right now. My seed is already altering your DNA. GarLycans will know what I've done within hours or days, depending on the strength of the bond. They'll smell it and sense it from you. Lycans and Vampires will as well. You won't be safe in the human world. You'll have to live with your pack so they can protect you. It's done, Angel." He took her hand again with his, clasping them both once more.

She didn't know what to say or think. It was the shock.

"It's my seed that starts the change while in fluxing and I was in the claiming. It's so you are able to breed with me easier, and hormones were released to make you mine. The good news is that you don't have to worry about human years. Not for at least twenty or so years, when you'll start to age again. Surviving mates keep those traits for about that long. You'll be the same physically, as far as strength and your abilities go, but you'll have a better immune system and heal a little faster. Remain very still when you have cuts. That's how we mend wounds."

"Surviving mates? Why did you say that?"

"I'm going to fall. Lord Aveoth would only kill or enslave you to ensure my suffering."

"What the hell does fall mean?"

"It's when we fly so high that the air thins until we can't breathe and change into human form. We fall." He clamped his lips together.

Dread and understanding hit. "You'll die. No one could survive that."

"That's the point. It's an honorable end to our existence. It will keep you safe. As I said, you need to tell whatever guardian that replaces me that I forced you to—"

"No!" Angel shook her head. "Stop it. You're not going to do this fall thing. No fucking way."

"It's the only way to keep you safe. As I said, it's an honor to fall for you. I will—"

"Will not do that." She released his hands and sat up, getting in his face. She grabbed a handful of his hair at the base of his neck so he couldn't pull away. "No, Creed. I'll go away and not come back. When is your hundred years up? You just said I'll live longer. Nobody will know what happened here unless they smell me. I'll go back to Seattle today."

"I can't lie. I have to report what happened."

"Bullshit!" She was furious. "I did this. Not you. You warned me you were losing control. I just thought you meant we might have rough sex. It

84

was an accident. This Lord Aveoth isn't perfect. No one is! Shit happens. We didn't plan this."

"I have honor, Angel. I must confess the truth of having a mate to Lord Aveoth."

"And I have this thing called common sense, and wanting to save both of our asses if your laws are that messed up. No." She shook her head. "I won't let you commit suicide. Do you got that? Not an option. Forget about it. We're going to go with my plan. I'm going to jump in my rental and haul ass to the airport to fly out of here. You're going to keep being guardian here until your time is up. Then we're going to pretend we mated after you come get me. See? No one's the wiser and no broken laws. Doesn't that sound like a plan?"

"Come get you?"

She nodded. "I'm your mate. Don't think I'm going to let you forget that. I'm willing to wait for you."

Creed wrapped his arm around her waist and pulled her closer. It smashed her breasts against his chest when she almost fell into him. He reached around her with his other arm and hooked her under her ass, dragging her closer. He took a seat and adjusted her body until she sat on his lap.

"I'm glad you were the one, Angel. You've always been my weakness. That's why I stayed away when you said you had feelings for me. I knew I couldn't resist if you touched me. I wanted to bring you home and live in your warmth. You are life and everything that matters to me."

Tears swam in her eyes. "Now you're going to be all lovey and wonderful. Damn it, Creed. Tell me we'll go with my plan."

85

"I must confess the truth to Lord Aveoth that I have a mate. I could never live with a lie that big."

"Then I'll go with you. We'll do this together."

He reached up and forced her to release his hair. He brought her fingers to his lips and brushed a kiss over the back of them. "No. I won't risk your life or them enslaving you."

Tears slipped down her cheeks. "I've loved you for as long as I can remember. I won't survive if you do this fall thing. Do you understand? Especially now that you're mine." She leaned her head against his chest. "You *are* mine. Not anyone else's."

He rested his chin on the top of her head. "Not according to my people. I had no right to take a mate. I broke the law. The fact that we didn't mean to form this bond won't matter. We're ruthless with laws for a reason. I've always understood that."

She realized he was as stubborn as ever. She had to go and fall in love with someone like Creed. It meant she had to accept there were some things she couldn't change about him, even if right now, she really wished she could. "Fine. You go take your lashes and be locked in some dark hole for ten years, but know I'll be waiting for you when you get out. Does that mean you're totally free when you're released?"

"Yes, but Lord Aveoth could kill you, and you are too kindhearted to survive being enslaved. Did I not explain what would happen?"

"My ass will be in Seattle. Don't worry about me. Just come for me when you're done being noble."

"They'd send scouts from my clan after you."

"Fine. I won't be in Seattle. I can get lost for ten years. I've gotten to know the human world really well since I've been living with them." She curled into him. "I can take care of myself. I'll let my parents know where I am when you get out so you can find me, or I can come to you. It will be tough keeping them in the dark for that long but they'll be safer if they don't have a way of telling anyone where I am."

"It would be too dangerous for you if you left the pack. Any Vampire or Lycan will know you're a mate. We're feared by most, and you will smell like me."

"Like being a vessel to any asshole would be better, if your lord doesn't take off my head. I can handle avoiding suckheads and tail chasers."

He chuckled when he leaned his head down.

She met his gaze. "What?"

"You grew up with Lycans. Tail chasers?"

"It's accurate. Have you seen young Lycans play? Or our men on the hunt for a woman to nail? My parents think it's cute that I call them that. The others, not so much. I live in Seattle. Do you know what we have there?"

"What?"

"Lots of rain and people, but also lush green spaces. It's a playground for Vampires and Werewolves. I already avoid both. My parents kept reaching out to the packs there to look after me and possibly find me a mate. That got old real fast. I avoid clubs and anywhere a lot of people hang out, since the blood hunters think those are all-you-can-eat buffets. Humans have their own predators. Those are the toughest things I deal with. Human-on-human crime is way out of control, yet I've survived just fine. I only had to send one person to the hospital. I never saw any guardians there, and believe me, I always watch the skies at night." She wouldn't admit she had hoped to spot him.

"You could get hurt."

"You seem determined to go home to tell your Lord Aveoth what happened between us. I know I'd be wasting my breath trying to talk you into keeping silent. I get that. Unlike you, my head doesn't fill with rocks." She smiled at him to soften her words. "I also don't want to find myself chained down by anyone unless you're the one doing it. That means this is the only option we have so we can be together again one day." A horrible thought struck. "Nobody ever dies from this encasing thing, do they?"

"Not to my knowledge. I'll survive. I'm young and strong."

She hated knowing what he'd go through. "Are you sure I can't talk you into running away with me? We could find some tiny town with like ten human residents. Nobody would look for us there. Ever want to take up farming? I could probably learn how to grow corn or something. You could chase off the crows. We'll find somewhere super flat with no mountains within a hundred miles. That way we'll know none of your people could be our neighbors."

He smiled. "You always amuse me with your silly suggestions."

"What's wrong with corn?" She tossed off the brave front. "I wouldn't care where we lived or what we did to survive as long as I have you."

The sad look returned to his eyes. "You really do love me."

"I always have." She knew he'd probably never be able to say the same words to her. He had her on his lap though, holding her. Emotion shone in his eyes when he was looking at her. He felt things for her. She believed that. It was enough. He'd admitted she was his weakness. That was almost equal to love from a GarLycan with mostly Gargoyle traits.

"I concede to you on your first plan."

"Where you go be noble and I don't get caught until you're freed?"

"That one."

Her heart was breaking. She tried to hide the pain. Creed was her mate. She'd just found that out, only to lose him. It was almost too cruel. Ten years would seem like an eternity but in the end, he'd come for her.

"I have a question."

"Of course you do. You're always curious, Angel."

"Just please tell me we're going to have sex when you find me, and that I won't have to wait until your next ravaging thing. That's really going to suck if being mated to you means only getting you naked with me every three decades. It's not a deal breaker, but I'm warning you that I'll be buying batteries. I'll also probably make you watch just to see if you get turned on enough to want to join me."

"Batteries?"

"Oh, come on. You have a television. I saw it in the other room. Batteries. As in, I own a vibrator. Know what one of those are? Don't you ever watch porn? I thought all men did. I know Lycans do."

The color of his eyes bled silver. "You do?"

89

"Watch porn? Not really, but I do own a vibrator. I'll show you when you get out of prison." She paused. "Those are words I never thought would come out of my mouth. It proves how much I love you. Now stop avoiding my question. Do you only want to have sex when you're ravaging?"

"You're my mate."

"And is that a yes, we're going to have sex often, or your way of working up to telling me that I'm just going to have to deal with it because I'm signed on to being with you?"

He chuckled. "I can't ignore your touch."

She opened her hand and lightly slapped his chest. "Now you're purposely talking in riddles. Give me a straight answer."

He pulled his arm out from under her knees and she gasped when he slid it between her thighs, cupping her pussy. He rubbed his hand across her clit, back and forth. She was still wet from them having sex. He was teasing her and it felt really good. She moaned.

"Does that answer your question?"

"I don't know. You seem to like being mean to me sometimes."

He pulled his hand away from her pussy and she clenched her teeth.

"I guess you being my mate doesn't dull your asshole attitude any, huh?"

"Get up and find out." He forced her to stand when he gripped her hips, lifting her.

She stared at his groin. He was getting hard. She backed up toward the bed. "That looks promising."

He arched one eyebrow—and then lunged.

He could move fast, and she didn't have time to even try to dodge his outstretched arms, not that she wanted to. He grabbed her around her middle and her feet were jerked right off the floor. He rolled and she landed half on him, half on the bed. Creed adjusted, coming down fully on top of her.

She opened her mouth but his kiss made her forget what she had meant to say. Her arms wrapped around his neck. He had a fantastic mouth. He pulled away before she could really explore him. His eyes were so beautiful that she couldn't look away when he stared at her.

"You touch me and I feel more than I ever have. I can't resist you. Is that clear enough? I can't build a shield strong enough to keep you out. You're a part of me."

"I'm glad. Are you mad at me?"

"No. Never at you. It's the situation and the danger it puts you in that sent me into a rage. I won't allow you to be hurt, Angel."

"The situation could be better. I want to protect you, too. We should strengthen the bond between us." She tilted her head to the other side, exposing the shoulder he hadn't bitten. "Do that fusion thing."

"Fluxing?"

"Yeah. That."

He frowned.

"What? Do you think I can't handle seeing you that way with my eyes open and when I'm not coming down from how good you make me feel? I can. I accept everything about you, Creed. I love you when you're in skin and when you're a bit stony. I love your eyes, regardless of what color they are. I even think you're cute when you're grumpy as hell and brooding."

His features softened.

"Get hard for me, baby," she teased. "Bring on the gray and the wings."

He hesitated. "No."

That stabbing sensation to her heart wasn't expected. So much for her thinking he wouldn't be able to reject her in any way, now that they'd mated.

"Don't look at me that way. I plan to strengthen our bond, but not until after this is over."

"Why? We're mated. We might as well make it a strong bond." She tried not to feel hurt.

"Gargoyles can sense and track their mates for long distances. Our bond isn't strong. It means you'd have an easier time going out range and making it very difficult for me to find you."

"You're saying that like it's a good thing."

"It would be tragic if Lord Aveoth decides to use me to hunt for you. It's called the glooming. It's when a mate is critically or fatally wounded, and he automatically tries to reach his mate. They used to do it the old days in Europe, when some of the clans fought amongst themselves. It's how they located their enemies' fortresses. They would seize a mated male and wound him so badly that he couldn't think through the pain. It was instinct to go to his mate. They'd just follow him and attack."

"That's really messed up."

"Yes. It's also why I'm waiting to strengthen our bond."

"What's your range now?"

He rolled away from her and climbed off the bed.

"Where are you going?"

"A test. I need to know. Don't move." He left the room.

She sat up and crossed her legs, her attention fixated on the doorway. He was gone for several long minutes. He didn't look happy when he returned. He'd also put on jeans.

"Well?"

"It's stronger than I thought. I went to the mouth of my home and could tell exactly where you were. I would say a hundred miles right now. Maybe two. Not more than that."

"That's a lot of miles."

"Once our bond is strong, I could track you across a few states. See why I consider it short range?"

"I do." She reached out to him. "Come here. I'm not done with you."

He didn't come closer. "It's time, Angel. We don't have any more of it left."

"You said you'd go tonight. We still have today."

"That was before I checked my voicemail. It seems the elders were worried when you weren't returned to your parents by morning, the way I'd indicated you would be. They left messages on my phone that I didn't hear, since I'd left it outside. The elders must have called my people. I have a message from Lord Aveoth to call him immediately or he's sending

93

scouts this way. It seems your pack believes I may have accidently killed you."

Her mouth dropped open. "Give me your phone."

"I left it outside and away from the entrance. I rarely bring it in. Signals can be tracked."

"I didn't see it out there when I was looking for it when I thought you were hurt."

"It's about a hundred yards to the right and a hundred feet up a crevice, near my outdoor shower. You wouldn't have. I don't keep it where it will lead someone right to my door."

She eyed his jeans. "And those? Where were those hiding?"

"Under the couch cushions. It works well to store clothing out of sight so I'm not staring at them in a pile on the floor. I don't have a closet or a lot of drawer space."

It hit her then. She wouldn't see him for a long time. *Ten years.*

She scrambled off the bed and threw her arms around his waist, pressing her cheek against his chest. He seemed stunned but then he put his arms around her to hold her tight.

"This is so unfair. I know life isn't but this really sucks." She wanted to cry.

"The time will pass and I will find you. Don't go where you've been. It will be the first place they look. I have something for you."

She lifted her chin. "What?"

"First, you need to get dressed."

"Can we shower together?"

"No. I want them to smell sex on you. It will fool your pack into thinking that's why they might pick up my scent. The Lycan elders seem to have Lord Aveoth on speed dial," he grimly stated. "They can't figure out we've mated or they'll call him right away."

He eased his hold and backed away, leaving her no choice but to let him go. He motioned her to follow him into the bathroom, where he reached up to a crevice she hadn't seen before. He brought down a first-aid kit. He withdrew gauze and a cream, then medical tape. "This will hide your blood scent. They can't suspect I bit you. Leave immediately, Angel. Lord Aveoth might have already ordered scouts this way. They could arrive as early as tonight. I will refuse to speak until I'm brought before him. That will give you time to get to the airport and take the first flight out. Don't tell me where. Don't tell anyone. I'll be fine as long as I know you're safe. Know that, my heart."

He called her his heart. She fought tears. He was being so sweet. His hands were gentle as he cleaned away all the blood from her skin and lathered on the thick, goopy cream over her bite marks, then bandaged it. She noticed that the marks she'd given him were completely gone. He'd healed.

She followed him into his bedroom again, and he withdrew a large T-shirt. She took it, putting it on. It fell to her thighs. He was much taller. She knew she'd keep it with her until they met again, just to have something of his. He bent, pulling out a pair of his boxer briefs. They were black with a quality name brand.

"I don't need anything with a flap."

He smiled. "Wear them anyway. I have to visit the elders and your alpha, so I'm going to drop you off at your home. I won't allow anyone to see that lovely ass of yours except me."

She put them on. They were more comfortable than she'd thought they'd be, and looked like long shorts since the bottoms showed about an inch below where the shirt fell. He took her hand and she followed him into the living room.

He picked up a small black backpack off the couch. It hadn't been there before. He released her hand. "Turn."

"What is that?"

"It's for emergencies. Every guardian keeps one stashed when they're assigned to protect a Lycan pack, in case we have to leave in a hurry. We've been attacked before, and it's standard to keep a bag if we need to blend with humans."

It was heavy. "Don't you need it?"

"Not where I'm going. It's money and some spare clothes. I want you to have them with you. The money will help you survive and my scent is on the clothing, so a part of me will remain with you."

She was going to bawl. She fought it. He was being brave but then again, he was a pro at hiding his feelings. The fact that he was being sweet made it worse, as if he were intentionally trying to show her that he had a tender side. She'd fair better if he barked orders at her and was his normally chilly self.

"Let's go."

"No shirt?"

"They'll only destroy it when I take the lashes."

She closed her eyes and turned her head, fighting tears.

"Shush." He pulled her into his arms. "This is temporary. It's only ten years. We'll have a future to look forward to together."

She clung to him. "I love you."

"You are my only weakness, Angel."

That was as good as saying he loved her.

He pulled away. "We must go. Our time is shorter by the second to make your plan work. I was informed when I checked in last that some of my clan would be not too far from this area for a few days. It won't take them that long to reach us if they plan to come."

She wiped her eyes, then lowered her hands. A sniffle wasn't bad, considering she was heading toward a full-on breakdown as soon as she crossed the Alaska state line. She stared into his eyes.

"Okay."

"You are my brave Angel."

"You're mine too, so forget all about that fall thing. Swear to me on your honor. No falling."

"I swear." No hesitation. "Let's go."

He didn't wait, just scooped her into his arms. She clung to him as he strode toward the exit. She glanced one last time at his home. They'd never be back. She fought the anguish that thought caused.

He spread his wings once they were outside.

"Our parting must be formal. It's what they will expect if anyone is watching for us. Tell them the backpack is yours if they ask. They didn't see me pick you up. I made certain you weren't followed. That's why I was already in the woods. I wanted to make sure you got there safely."

"I understand."

He paused and looked down at her. "I will think of you every second."

He does love me. He just didn't have the words.

He bent his knees and leapt. The falling sensation made her feel a little queasy, but then they were soaring over the river. She loved the feel of the wind against her body and being held by Creed. She turned her head and quickly placed a kiss on his cheek.

"I'm going to miss you so much. I love you."

He turned his head, the silver in his eyes flaring. "You're my Angel. Now be my brave one. The elders are gathered."

She turned her head, spotting the village. He was right. There was a small group near the shoreline. She swallowed hard.

"Ice cold. Got it. Did I mention how amazing you are in bed?"

He actually missed a beat with his wings and they fell a few feet before he recovered. "Now you're being a naughty Angel."

"Wait until we're together again. I'm going to have ten years to think up everything I plan to do to you. There's going to be a lot of sex."

He growled. "Stop. I can't arrive with a hard-on."

She smiled. "Okay. You're shit in bed then, and I'll have to train you. It will be torture having to fuck you until you get it right."

His lips twisted for a split second, almost a smile. "I'm going to miss you too."

The wind helped dry the tears that sprang into her eyes. She rapidly blinked them back. "Here we go. Put on your Gargoyle face, baby."

"You too. You're my mate. Never let them see your pain."

She masked her features. She could do it. He flew over the elders and dropped to the ground in front of her parents' house. He was slow to lower her. She was slower to release his neck. He backed up until she had no choice.

She had to clear her throat. "Thank you."

"Thank you."

They stared at each other, and then he bowed his head, turning away. He strode toward the elders. The door to the cabin behind her opened and she forced herself to stop watching Creed.

Her mother looked worried. "Are you okay? I told everyone you were fine, that Creed wouldn't hurt you, but the elders and Alpha Picoz thought he'd murdered you."

"I'm in one piece." *Hold it together.* She walked up the porch steps and gripped her mom's arm. "Let's go inside. I feel watched."

"You are. Everyone was abuzz when the elders came here this morning at nine to see your condition. They were worried, since this time it was a human who'd volunteered."

Her father waited inside. He sniffed at her and growled. "Are you okay? Did he hurt you?"

"I'm great," she lied.

"Where did you get the backpack?" Her mother eyed it. "It smells of outside but not of you."

"It *was* outside." Creed seemed to keep half his stuff hidden on the mountain outside of his home. She tried to think up a lie. "I brought it with me last time and I forgot it in the woods. I remembered it last night, when I was going to meet with Creed, so I grabbed it. You know how I love to go read. It's just some books. I'd stashed it between some of those rocks I love to sit on, to keep it dry when it rained, and forgot about it."

Her mother motioned to her father. He seemed grateful to flee into the family room. Her mom studied her face too intently. "Are you really okay?"

"I am." Some of her emotions bled through. "You know how I feel about Creed. We expected it to be tough on me that this was only a one-night thing. He's amazing." None of that was a lie.

"The sex?"

"Just like you said it would be and so much more."

Her mother smiled. "I'm glad you had that. You might want to shower. I know your nose isn't as sensitive but even Lycan girls wash off a man's scent afterward, before they come home. You smell like Creed—and everything you did. Go on. I bet you're hungry. I'll make food."

Not quite everything we did. "I'm not hungry but thanks. I'm going to go to my room and clean up." She fled down the hallway.

She hadn't taken the time to unpack much so it was easy to shove her things back into the pack she'd brought. She left out a pair of jeans and a sweater, after donning on a bra and panties. She packed Creed's borrowed things and then hesitated. It would hurt her parents if she just left without saying goodbye. She just couldn't tell them the real reason why she was leaving.

100

There were pack rules, and fine lines she wouldn't have her parents cross. This was their home, the people who they lived with every day. She wouldn't put them in a difficult position.

She shoved the straps for both packs over one shoulder, the good one that wasn't bandaged, and grabbed the keys for the rental off the dresser. One deep breath later and she followed the sound of her parents' voices into the kitchen.

"Why do you have your bags?" Her mother scowled.

"My boss left a message for me. He's going to fire me if I don't get back by morning. I'm so sorry. I have go."

"I didn't hear it ring." Her mother sighed. "You're running away from Creed again."

She hated to lie to the two people who had raised her but she had to. They would have to tell Alpha Picoz if she admitted she was Creed's mate. It would get her parents into hot water if they hid that knowledge, even for the hour it would take her to be far from their territory.

"It didn't ring. I can get emails on my phone. I told you he wasn't happy when I took the sick days, but now half the staff has come down with the flu. Humans get sick so easy. I can't lose my job." She walked over to her father and hugged him. "I love you, Dad." He embraced her back and planted a kiss on the top of her head. She turned to her mother next. "I'm so sorry to leave like this. I love you, Mom."

Her mom growled, showing her irritation. "You could have at least showered."

"I will when I get home."

"You smell like sex," her mother whispered. "It could draw males to you."

"I'm flying with a bunch of humans. They won't know." She faked a smile. "I don't plan on getting real close to them anyway if the flu is going around. I don't want to catch it. Love you. I'll call you when I'm home safe."

They hugged once more and Angel fled. There was no sign of Creed, her alpha or the elders when she shoved her things onto the passenger-side floor and started the engine.

Her gaze lifted to the sky. Were scouts from his clan about to show up when it grew dark? She put on her belt and backed up. It was tough to drive slow until she reached the main road.

It was key that she get far away so Creed didn't feel the need to play hero by offering to give up his life for hers. Her hands fisted on the wheel in a death grip until she left the village. She floored it then. Her gaze kept sweeping the sky. It wasn't like GarLycans often flew in broad daylight, but her pack's territory was remote enough that they might risk it.

She wanted to cry but she resisted. With her luck, she'd wreck the SUV and never get out of Alaska. Creed would be told she'd been captured, and then they wouldn't have a future at all. *I can do this for him.*

Chapter Seven

Creed stared at Joe with a bored expression. The two-hundred-and-ninety-seven-year-old Lycan elder seemed to enjoy the sound of his voice as he droned on about the importance of being respectful of traditions and their alliance.

Alpha Picoz stood and lifted a hand. "Enough, Joe." He stepped closer to Creed. "We were worried about the girl. She's a part of this pack but she's not Lycan. It's a courtesy that we even ask our women to accommodate your needs. It was agreed upon that we'd have her follow your ritual, fully expecting you to follow it as well. You stated you'd have her returned first thing in the morning. The fact that she's human is—"

Creed stopped listening to the alpha when his senses alerted him to one of his own kind. The door to the meeting hall creaked open and he turned. Kelzeb entered as if he owned the place. The lead enforcer of Lord Aveoth—and the man Creed reported to—wore all black clothing. He glanced around before fixing his stare directly on Creed.

"Is she alive?"

Creed noticed some of the Lycans winced. It was their sensitive hearing. Kelzeb had a deeper voice than most found pleasant. He knew the question was directed at him, so he answered. "Yes."

"Damaged?"

"No."

Kelzeb crossed his arms and slid his gaze to the alpha. "So what's the big stink? I could hear what you were saying all the way from where I parked my Jeep. You should close the windows if you don't want just anyone hearing what's going on inside. You've drawn a crowd."

"He didn't return her when expected."

Kelzeb sighed. "So?"

Alpha Picoz snarled. "So? He said—"

"Enough," Kelzeb thundered.

The Lycans all whined from the sound, protecting their ears. Creed didn't know why Lord Aveoth's enforcer spoke that way to the pack, but he didn't care either.

Kelzeb lowered his voice. "It's the ravage. It's not on a schedule like when the sun rises and sets. Hormones are a bitch. Do I really need to explain that to anyone in this room? You're all in heat for...how long? Days? Weeks? I don't really give a damn. That wasn't a question. The girl was returned alive and undamaged. Case closed."

Alpha Picoz snarled again. "We care. We allow our women to help the guardian through his time of need. The least—"

"Allow?" Kelzeb thundered again. "Is that what you said? It's part of the agreement between our clan and your pack that you ask for volunteers, if whoever we assign to protect your ass goes through the ravage while he's on duty. Did he steal one of your women? Kidnap her?" He pinned Creed with a glare. "Did you swoop from the sky and grab one of them while she was kicking and screaming to be put down?"

"No."

Kelzeb threw his arms wide. "There you go. She agreed to it and she's fine. I had to drive all the way here for this? Do you know how much that

104

irritates me? I had better things to do today." He glared at the alpha. "Then I find you grilling a GarLycan as if he answers to you. He doesn't. Should I remind you how many packs would jump at the chance to have a GarLycan guardian? He took one night off and, apparently, all of the morning. He's not on duty during the daylight hours. Hell, he can fuck *all* of your unmated women anytime he wants if they are willing. There's nothing in your laws that forbids them from freely making that choice. He's not a monk, or your personal whipping boy when you're in a bad mood. We're done here." Kelzeb spun. "Let's go, Creed."

Creed followed without glancing at the Lycans around him. The enforcer bypassed the Jeep he'd arrived in and headed directly toward the river. It meant he wanted to have a private chat. They stopped at the water's edge and Kelzeb glanced around, his eyes narrowed.

"What a bunch of old women," Kelzeb muttered. He crossed his arms and finally looked at Creed. "Why were you standing in there listening to them? You know you don't have to. Tell them to piss off and fly back home. They are lucky you're here. They can bitch all they want, but bottom line, I knew this was going to be a waste of time. You've had this assignment long enough to know not to cross any lines that would cause real tension with the alliance."

"I was later than I told them I would be."

"So you thought you'd take that shit? You're more patient than I am. I would have told them my dick is none of their concern, nor what I do with it, as long as she's willing. I know you, Creed. You'd never take something that wasn't freely offered."

Creed shrugged. "They are driven by their emotions. I've adjusted to that. It makes them feel as if they have some control over my duties when I listen. It's mildly annoying but tolerable. It keeps the peace."

Kelzeb grinned. "You're a better man than I." His humor faded fast. "Is there anything you want to tell me?"

"I need to seek an audience with Lord Aveoth immediately. I am flying in tonight."

"About what?"

"I will only speak of it with Lord Aveoth."

"I see." Kelzeb cocked his head. "So, she was human, huh?"

"Yes."

"I only know of one human who lives with this pack. I thought she moved away. Seattle, wasn't it?"

"She visits her parents." Creed's spine stiffened. He didn't like that his clan kept tabs on Angel or her whereabouts.

"I'd like to meet her."

Creed grew very still inside. He couldn't lie and he hoped she was already gone. It had been a good half an hour or more since he'd seen her. "I dropped her off at her parents' home. It is the fourth cabin from the main trail to the river. White porch with two rocking chairs."

"I didn't drive all the way from our clan. I was a few hours from here, visiting this pack that has an abundance of unmated females. Didn't you get the update?"

"I wasn't certain which of our clan would be in the area, or the exact location. I was only warned there might be flight traffic that wasn't hostile."

"A few of the Lycan alphas in the states want to make deals for guardians. I'm sure they were encouraged by their elders, since they know about the sweet deal this pack gets from us. Word spread that we keep their woods clear of those pesky poachers who like to sneak around at night, setting traps and taking potshots at wolves. They've also had some issues with Vampires and were told there are none left in this area, since we cleared them out. They want alliances with us and aren't above using their women to get them. There were a few I approved to make the trip to meet our single men, but I still have a few other packs to visit. I hate these bullshit gigs. Good thing I'm only sent on them a few times a year."

Creed said nothing. He could understand why another pack would wish to align with his clan. Lycans couldn't protect their territory as well as someone could from the sky. A guardian was able to cover large areas quickly and take out threats before they reached the pack homes.

"I like Lycan women. Don't get me wrong. My mother is one. The thing is, I'm finding myself drawn to another type lately. Aveoth is kept busy with his Jill. She was raised totally human. The things that come out of her mouth amuse me. She has an issue with authority, so Aveoth is constantly having to deal with her antics." He chuckled. "It looks lively. She has only a small understanding of what we are, so she has no fear. It's refreshing. I want to see if this Angel stirs my blood. She survived a night with you during the ravage so I know she's sexually compatible with our kind."

107

Creed managed to remain still when he really wanted to attack the other GarLycan. Angel was *his*. Suddenly he considered Kelzeb a threat. They had been friendly in the past but he'd kill him if he laid a finger on his mate.

"What do you think? Would this Angel consider mating with a GarLycan?"

He chose his words carefully. "She's a human who was raised with a Lycan pack. She holds no prejudices against our kind."

Kelzeb grinned. "You're good. Not even an eye twitch or hint of anger in your voice. You even answered without giving anything away."

"What do you believe I would hide?"

Kelzeb leaned in closer and his expression grew serious. "I decided to take a little look around before I drove in. Get a lay of the land, because it's been some years since I've been here. My first stop was your place. You didn't cover the opening, Creed. You've grown a bit lax about security, living with these Lycans, since they can't reach your lair. The mountain is too sheer for them to climb. You should have burned the bedding with her blood on it. You bit her, didn't you? I doubt some virgin would climb into bed with one of us, and it was near the top of the bed, not the bottom where you would have chained her."

Creed said nothing but his heart pounded.

"That's what I thought." Kelzeb shook his head. "Damn it, Creed. I knew the second I saw that blood and where it was that you didn't chain her down. You mated her."

"I did chain her down." That he could truthfully say.

"Then how in the hell did her blood get near the top of your bed? What is she? Ten or eleven feet tall?"

Creed heard Kelzeb's sarcastic tone.

"So you chained her but then let her go. You're planning on going to see Aveoth tonight. That implies you have something to tell him. You could have accidently scratched her with your fingernails, but it must be more than that for you return to our cliffs. Why won't you tell me what happened?"

Creed just coldly regarded him.

"Damn. I'm trying to put myself in your place. You, for whatever reason, released her from the chains and bit her. Did she beg you to take her the way Lycan men do? Did she freak the hell out in the chains so you showed compassion? Say something!"

Creed kept his lips sealed.

"Was it just a cut somehow or did you mate her?"

Silence.

"I'm going to have to go to her parents' house and meet her. Is that what you want? I'll do it. It's my job to investigate what went down here after this pack called Aveoth. He wants a report."

"I'll report to him myself."

"Just tell me what the hell happened. I might be able to help."

Creed debated the wisdom of seeking an ally. He knew Lord Aveoth and Kelzeb were close friends. He also knew the man in front of him had a reputation for being lax about the rules. It wasn't a secret that Kelzeb had been punished by the previous lord of their clan for many infractions. As a youth, the lead enforcer had liked to test limits and push boundaries.

He'd also admitted he had an attraction to humans. It was worth the risk.

"I am still in service to Lord Aveoth until my hundredth birthday."

"You *did* mate her. Damn. He'll want to see her, too, when you go before him."

"She is not at fault." He wanted that made clear. "The punishment is mine to take."

"You know it doesn't work that way. She's your mate, and you technically belong to the clan. It means you're both considered one unit now. You go before Aveoth with her at your side."

"I will not risk her being killed or enslaved. I told her to remain here with her pack so they could protect her." It wasn't a lie. He *had* told her that.

"Oh, fuck. Her pack can't overrule our laws. She stopped belonging to them the second you mated her. She's one of ours now. Just answer me this: Did you plan to mate her or was it one of those moments when your dick did the thinking for you?"

"I did not plan it."

"Did you untie her because she was scared? Were you too rough? I would worry about fucking one of them, and I'm not suffering the ravage. It's not as if we're known for being gentle in bed to begin with. I get how it could happen. You were trying to console her and one thing led to a moment of insanity. Do you even like her? Hell. What a mess."

"I regret the timing, not that she's mine."

Kelzeb cocked his head, peering at him with interest. "You live here and have known her for a while. How close are you to her?"

There was no reason to deny it. "I feel for her."

"Are you in love with her?"

"I will fall for her to keep her safe, if it comes down to it."

"Just say you love her. You're telling me you'll die before you let her suffer any punishment."

"I feel for her," he repeated.

"Damn. Your father must be proud of you. I'm a big disappointment to mine. He barely withstands my presence. He doesn't like the way I talk or that I'm not...well, like you."

"It's a difficult balance with Gargoyle fathers and Lycan mothers. I know we're both first-generation half-breeds."

"That's a nice way to put it. I enjoy it when my mother slaps the shit out of my father for the things he says to her. I almost envy her. I'd love to deck the bastard from time to time. It's the only enjoyment I get out of these road trips. He's not able to glower at me from a distance since I don't run into him."

"Solitude helps."

Kelzeb turned his head, glancing up at the lair, then back at Creed. "But the girl visits you. You let her up there."

"Just for the ravage."

"First time? What about when you take lovers?"

"I don't."

111

"Shit. You've been assigned this post for about three decades, give or take some years. Never?"

"No."

Kelzeb closed his eyes and shook his head. "Damn." He reached up and ran his fingers through his hair and looked at Creed with sympathy. "I didn't know. Why the hell didn't you get friendly with the locals?"

"There were no unattached females of age when I arrived. And I stay solely in this territory unless I am called home to give updates to you. Later, the desire wasn't there." He paused. "The only woman I wanted was the one I knew I couldn't have. She deserved more than just sharing my bed from time to time. It would have been too difficult for us both."

"Angel."

He inclined his head. "She wanted a mate. I couldn't give her that."

"So you decided to pick her last night? Why? You had to know she was the one who might make you lose control."

"I believed I could resist, and…"

"And what? Just spit it out."

"I couldn't hurt her that way. It would have been painful for her to know I had chosen another when she'd volunteered. I already made her suffer by rejecting her when she approached me to be my mate. It's why she left here in the first place. After she was gone, she visited every year. There would have been talk if I'd taken a lover, and she would have heard. I didn't want to add to her pain."

"You really do love her. You've had it bottled up for years. You need to tell Aveoth this. He's not such a bad guy. Go pack an overnight bag and

112

I'll swing by the girl's parents' place to tell her to do the same. We'll drive home together. It's best if we just get this over with. I'll speak to Aveoth privately first, and then you need to be open with him. Tell him you've loved her for years and did everything you could to resist. We've all suffered the ravage."

"She won't be coming with us."

"She will. He's got a soft spot for humans since Jill. Aveoth has never killed a woman or had one enslaved since he became our lord. Those were just bullshit rumors circulating, that he murdered his lover. Lane came to him already broken in spirit, and it was only a matter of time before she couldn't live with the pain she felt. She leapt off that ledge of her own free will."

"He challenged his own father and took leadership. Lord Aveoth is ruthless."

Kelzeb shook his head. "I'm going to share something with you that stays right here on this spot. Am I clear?"

"Yes."

"Your word?"

"Given."

"Lord Abotorus was one cold bastard. Aveoth and I never trusted our fathers, so we would eavesdrop on council sessions they held together. We were listening when Lord Abotorus and the council decided adding Lycan bloodlines to our clan had been a mistake. They were plotting to murder the Lycan mates—and all the children the Gargoyles had with them. That included me, Aveoth, you, and your brothers, if I need to point that out. *That's* when Aveoth challenged to be lord. We told the clan what

113

they were plotting recently, but not the exact details of how we discovered what they were up to. Here's another secret. Ever wonder what happened to Tuno and Yessa?"

"They were the only pure-blooded Gargoyle mated couple. They left to seek a life with another clan."

Kelzeb snorted. "Wrong. No mated pair leaves their young children behind. Elco and Winalin don't have parents because Lord Abotorus planned to replace his GarLycan mate with a Gargoyle one."

Creed let that sink in. "Yessa was already mated to Tuno."

"And she wanted to keep it that way. They died fighting side by side, making sure she didn't become a forced breeding vessel for that prick Abotorus. Both our fathers helped him attack them, but they fought to the death. We didn't know until after the fact. We saw them removing the bodies from the cliff and overheard enough to learn how they'd died. It's why Aveoth hasn't banished the siblings for their constant bad behavior and plotting. He feels guilt. They lost their parents because our fathers murdered them."

"The clan should have been told."

"It was our word against theirs back then. We couldn't follow them when they flew the bodies away, and had no idea where they'd disposed of them. Not to mention, what could anyone have done if we'd managed to prove it? Abotorus and the council were in charge. Aveoth had to challenge his father and kill him."

"I had no idea." Creed was stunned and horrified.

"Aveoth is nothing like his father. He's an excellent lord. His mother was an influence in his life. It means he has a heart...and occasionally

114

listens to it. I'm sympathetic to you and this Angel. There's a really good chance that he will be too."

"He'll have to make an example of me. Most would see it as a weakness on his behalf otherwise."

"Aveoth doesn't really give a damn about what others think of him. Anyone who's had doubts about his abilities to lead our people have met his sword. It tends to make an overall impression. He handpicked his enforcers. Do you know why he chose me as his first?"

"You're an old friend and an excellent fighter. He would trust you without question."

"I am and he knows I'd never betray him." Kelzeb nodded. "I'm also a half-breed. Most of his enforcers aren't full-bloods. He chose us because we're not like our fathers. We're loyal to him and we believe that change is needed for our survival. He took Jill as his mate. You live here, so you missed the fallout. There was a shit-storm over that in our clan. She's got human and VampLycan blood running through her veins. It means their younglings will carry slight Vampire bloodlines."

Creed tried to hide his surprise. "I wasn't aware." Vampires were their enemies, and while they'd made an alliance with the half-breed Lycans with Vampire bloodlines, they didn't mate with them. The full-blooded Gargoyles wouldn't stand for it. Their hatred had lived too long to accept them into their clan as members.

"Do you have a problem with Aveoth's mate?"

"No." He didn't like Vampires, but he hadn't spent centuries fighting with them until all he knew was that hatred.

"Good. You're not too much like your father then. Our fathers, along with the other two council members, tried to band together to strip Aveoth of his title after he mated Jill. They even demanded he leave our clan. They failed."

"I wasn't told."

"You should have been. Our fathers were smacked down hard and punished for their defiance."

"How?"

"Do you wish to seek vengeance for whatever your father suffered?"

"No. I'm only curious."

"I personally got a chuckle out of my old man being brought down. He's such a highhanded prick at times. They had to bow to Aveoth in front of everyone and apologize. They were stripped of their ranks in our clan. There's no more council of full-bloods. They hold no power and no longer have the ability to help enforce the laws they created. Aveoth allowed them to stay but all of them know they will be banished if they ever attempt to go against him again. He said he'd personally put them in a box and ship them back to one of the established clans in Europe."

Creed tried to imagine his father bowing and apologizing. "I wish I'd been there to see it."

"It was priceless." Kelzeb chuckled. "I whipped out my cell phone and shot a video. I got a few disapproving glares from some of our people but I don't care. I wanted to treasure that moment forever, after all the times my father has torn into my ass."

Creed felt a hint of envy. He could relate. His father had always disapproved of him. There had never been a time when he'd known pride from Kado. His father's superior attitude and haughtiness had been difficult at times.

"Are you ever resentful that your father swore you to duty for a hundred years?"

"Yes," Creed acknowledged. "It was done at my birth. I was raised in the lower caverns to begin my training young, before being sent out to guard the borders to the far north at the age of fifteen."

Kelzeb winced. "That's hell. No one is supposed to do more than a year. The council had you out there for about ten straight, didn't they? It's so damn cold it makes flying impossible most of the year. Why did you do it?"

"My father decided it would build character to keep offering to extend my assignment. He did it fourteen times in a row. Lord Aveoth realized how long I'd been there and reassigned me here. I believe he worried about my sanity."

"No shit. We would have pulled you sooner if we'd known, but it was the full-blood council who assigned most of those duties. Your father letting you live in a barren zone for all those years was flat-out cruel."

"Yes."

"That makes a lot of sense now, the one incident you caused. You are a guardian but spent all that time protecting nothing."

Creed frowned. "What incident? This is my first real offense."

"The human girl. It was a first for one of us, taking a human child and giving her to a Lycan pack. Your report stated she was abused and the situation was grim but it came as a surprise. Humans kill their children sometimes. It's sad but it's their problem. You made it ours. It was a big risk if the human authorities got involved. The full-blood council wanted to punish you for possibly exposing us to the outside world."

"Angel needed someone to help her." Creed was certain his father had been the one to lead that front. He'd received a harsh conversation after he'd filed that report. Kado had threatened to lash him himself but his mother had intervened. She'd ordered Creed to return to his assignment and had faced off against his enraged father. He'd stayed long enough to make certain she was in no danger.

He'd only seen his father in public after that. He was still unsure if he'd have bowed down to take that beating or if he'd have fought him. Though, he would have refused to hurt his mother by forcing her to watch her mate and one of her sons fight to the death.

"Aveoth agreed. We do watch human news. Saving a child from certain death is honorable. But now you've mated her. Does that feel strange?"

"I avoided her after I gave her to the couple who raised her. It wasn't until she was older that I spent time with her. I saw her spending a lot of time alone and it made me question my past actions, wondering if she was unhappy."

"The pack didn't take to her?"

"They did." Creed hesitated. "I hadn't taken into consideration that children eventually grow into adults when I brought her into this valley.

The elders and parents were training the adolescents how to hunt and adjust to the changes their bodies were going through."

"She wasn't a Lycan. I understand."

"They trained her how to fight but would leave her behind when they went into the woods. She couldn't keep up with them when they went on group runs." A memory surfaced. "Angel tried though. She's always been courageous, with a lot of spirit. At first some of the youths would stay with her, but she'd motion them on, not wanting to hold them back. Unfortunately, she had no sense of direction." He actually smiled. "She'd get lost on her own. That's when I first spoke to her again. She was sixteen and heading right into a bear's den. I prevented her from irritating a mother and her cubs."

"That would have been bad."

"Yes. It would have. I walked her back to the village to make certain she wouldn't get lost again. She asked me to go fishing with her. I resisted but she reminded me that I did have to eat. I still refused but then she started fishing in a spot I couldn't miss seeing from my lair. She seemed aware of it, because she'd do the funniest things, attempting to lure me to come down."

Kelzeb arched his eyebrows. "Like what?"

Creed smiled again. He couldn't not. "She'd do this thing she called a happy dance every time she caught a fish. She brought food with her sometimes, and would lift it up so I could see what she had and wave at me to join her. She even wrote on a big board she carried to that rock to tell me I was a stick in the mud. It amused me."

"And you caved."

His humor faded. "She drew me."

"You were attracted to her."

"She's so full of life. I started fishing with her. She'd bring food for us both, we'd talk. It was nice. Time passed and she matured. I noticed. She turned eighteen...and that's when the touching began."

"You touched her?"

"I allowed her to touch *me*. She was so curious."

"So this wasn't your first time having sex with her?"

"It was never like that. I wouldn't allow it. She wanted a mate, I couldn't give her that. She wasn't Lycan and considered sex something that only happened between two people in love. I allowed her to feel my wings. She wanted to see me in my other form, so I shelled for her. She told me I was beautiful."

Kelzeb grunted. "Not something we want to hear."

"It was a compliment. Fear was never my intention with her, and I was glad she approved of how I looked."

"Then she left?"

"She tried to initiate sex with me and told me what she felt in her heart. She said she would talk me into taking her as my mate. I removed myself from her and stayed away."

"You felt she had the power to break your will?"

Creed said nothing. Angel had become his one weakness.

"You're in love with her." Kelzeb sighed. "What a mess. But it's going to be okay. As I said, I'll talk to Aveoth when we get there before you have to make a formal audience. He'll cut you some slack. Especially after I

120

remind him of what you've been through because of your father. He can't stand Kado either."

"Thank you."

"Now, I'll go get the girl and you grab a bag. We don't have a lot of time."

"She's not here."

"Where is she?"

Creed hesitated. "I didn't want her to be punished and she didn't want me to fall. We compromised."

"What in the hell did you do?"

"She is my mate but her will is her own."

"Stop stalling. She's running, isn't she? Is that what you two worked out? She'd take off while you faced your punishment?"

"Yes."

"She'll smell like you." Kelzeb snarled. "It's going to put a target on her back."

"I'm aware and pointed that out to her. She has lived in the human world and feels confident that she can survive."

"Awww, fuck," Kelzeb hissed. "You bloody fool. She's got you wrapped around her damn finger. You're also still experiencing the tail end of the ravage. You're not thinking clear. I bet the first two things you were worried about were her being killed by Aveoth, and then how some bastard like one our fathers would turn her into a breeding vessel. This is the most vulnerable time for newly mated women. You're not the only one who will be able to track her. She's going through the change. She'll

121

be sending out pheromones for miles to anyone with a nose to pick up when her mate doesn't respond to her silent call to strengthen the bond. That's why we usually send new mates somewhere remote or have them stay in their homes. It's torment to the single males to smell how hot they get."

"She's human. That won't happen."

"I'm going to kick your father's ass myself! Kado never had the talk with you? It doesn't matter if she's human, Lycan, or a Gargoyle. It's going to happen to her. How strong was your bond?"

"Weak." Creed's father had told him it only happened with female Lycans and Gargoyles who mated to them. *Would he lie?*

"FUCK!" Kelzeb roared. He took a few ragged breaths, glaring at Creed. "She'll just feel a little warm and start to sweat. It won't alarm her but her scent will keep getting stronger until it spreads for miles. It's meant to draw you to her. It's nature's way of letting us know we need to strengthen that bond more. We can be a little resistant to feelings, so it turns on anything with a dick and a nose to pick it up. Old masters who ever spent time around our kind are going to identify it. They'll track her. Lycans will too. She's going to smell like the hottest bitch ever, and they'll lose their damn minds.

"They won't mean to kill her, but they will. I saw it happen once when I was in scout training and assigned to go on a mission to observe. A full-blood Gargoyle mated a Lycan and couldn't be bothered with forming more than a weak bond. He was negotiating an alliance with her pack. She started to put off the calling. The single males started to attack each other, fighting to the death to get to be the one to fuck her. She was injured but her mate flew off with her before she was raped. Six died. Either way, once it starts, your girl might as well have a neon spotlight over her head anywhere she goes that states 'fuck me'."

"My father would have told me."

"Unless Kado wanted to make certain you never mated a human—or got her killed by being ignorant, if you did. Now get your head out of your ass and remember what Vampires might do to her if she's captured. *They* won't kill her. They can heal whatever they do to her, and she won't change into one of them because she's your mate. They'll think she's the best torture toy ever. Call her on her cell phone and tell her to turn around."

"I...I don't have her number." Creed felt raw fear for Angel. "She's on her way to the airport." He turned, his wings ripping out of his back. It hurt like hell to change that fast but he had to get to her.

Kelzeb grabbed him. "No! She's probably had time to get out of the territory. It's broad daylight. You can't risk flying beyond this valley or you could be seen. No damn way are you ending up starring in a video clip on the internet. Aveoth *would* have your ass then. Get in my Jeep once you stop bleeding so you don't ruin my seats and I'll call two of our enforcers I left a few hours ago. They're out that way. They'll reach her if we don't."

Frustration nearly choked Creed. He hadn't been thinking clearly. He hadn't known Angel would put off the calling. "I'm going to *kill* my father. My mother isn't around anymore to be hurt by his death."

"I don't blame you. Put away the damn wings, Creed. That's an order."

He closed his eyes and tried to force his body into submission.

"Forget your overnight bag. I *told* Aveoth all of the guardians should come home for the ravage and bring a woman with them. This just proves it. Less fuck-ups happen if it's a more controlled environment. Let's go. I have spare clothes for you."

Chapter Eight

Angel fidgeted with the paper wrapped around the sandwich and took a sip of the soda she'd bought. She glanced up at the wall in the small airport. Her flight took off in forty minutes. Every second that passed seemed as if were ten.

Someone coughed near her and she tucked her head. It would be ironic if she caught some virus after lying to her mother. Karma could be a bitch. She took another bite of the sandwich. It wasn't bad, considering the vender worked from a refrigerated stand. She'd kill for a nice fast food joint or a good coffee shop, but they only boasted those in bigger airports.

I should have driven all the way to Anchorage.

She chewed on her lip, debating her choice all over again. She felt too emotional to drive that far and wanted out of Alaska as soon as possible. It's why she'd stopped in the first place.

All she could think about was Creed. *What is he doing? How is he feeling? Is he scared deep down inside to face his GarLycan lord?* She was terrified for him. He'd said he'd take lashes. *Does that mean what I think it does? Some asshole will whip him?* She lost her appetite.

She stood and felt a moment of dizziness. It passed fast as she located a trashcan and dumped the remainder of her food. The airport really needed to kick up the air conditioning. She glanced around. At least eight other passengers were waiting to crowd into a small plane to be taken to a larger airport to make their connections to wherever their destinations were.

She regretted wearing a sweater as she retook her seat, and tugged at the collar. She couldn't even remove it since she hadn't put on an undershirt in her haste to leave her parents' house. Sweat tickled along her back from the plastic seat. She shifted her ass into a more comfortable position, her gaze lowering to the two backpacks at her feet. She hadn't looked inside the one Creed had given her. She was afraid she'd totally lose it and start sobbing. Strangers didn't want to see that.

She sighed and closed her eyes, trying to think of her next move. The connecting flight in Anchorage would take her to Seattle. She needed to go home to pack her things before taking off. She kept some cash stashed in her kitchen but she'd need to hit the bank too, just to clear out her account. It could wait though. Priority one was making it home, and then leaving before anyone was sent after her.

GarLycans could only fly at night to avoid detection but they'd have to keep under the radar, literally. That would slow them down, since they had to avoid traveling by air over populated areas. She figured they wouldn't be able to reach her in Seattle until the next evening sometime, probably near dawn.

She looked at the clock on the wall, calculating. She'd have plenty of time if her connecting flight wasn't delayed. Her car had been left at the airport. She'd drive home and could clear out within a few hours, at most. She'd be long gone before dinnertime the following day.

Large cities were where Vampires thrived. Rural areas were more to the liking of Lycans. She'd have to find a safe middle ground.

More sweat irritated her and she reached down, lifting the hem of her sweater and getting some air to her stomach when she fanned the material. *It's summer still. Why did I put on a sweater? Oh, yeah. To hide the bite mark from my parents. It's hotter than hell in here.*

The desert. The thought popped into her head and she mulled it over. No one in her pack would want to live in some dinky town. Hot, flat, barren land with blasting temperatures and little to no outdoor water sources would put them off. Most humans didn't even like those kinds of conditions, so it meant not many would live there. It would be a stupid choice for a Vampire if he wanted to eat.

Okay. Death Valley, here I come. She was pretty sure that was somewhere in California. She'd have to look it up but it gave her a place to head in her car. She'd figure the rest out later.

Creed filled her thoughts again and she fought the urge to cry. He should have decided to run with her. She understood why he hadn't. He'd always been a straight shooter. He had a strong sense of honor. It was one of the many things she loved about him, but that didn't mean she didn't feel a little hurt that he'd picked doing the right thing over being with her. Ten years probably seemed like a drop in the bucket for his lifespan.

The prospect of spending the rest of her now-extended life with one man didn't frighten her. Her human friends were leery of even living with men. She'd been raised with Lycans though. Mating was forever. She'd always envied anyone who'd found the person they loved and wanted to be with. Now it seemed unfair that she'd spend her honeymoon phase on the run while Creed had to spend it in prison.

The woman across from her used her book to fan herself.

Angel sat up a little straighter. She was done. She needed to fit in and not draw attention to herself, but the way she was fidgeting would. She bent forward and lifted her backpacks. There was a bathroom across the small airport. It would only take a few minutes to switch into a T-shirt.

It was empty when she entered, and she washed her face then stripped off the sweater. She shoved it in with her other clothes and pulled out a thin cotton top. Her shoulder showed a little but it wouldn't matter. No human was going to even think she might have been bitten. They'd just assume it was a cut or scratch she'd bandaged. She used the bathroom and then exited.

The guy with short hair near the counter spun the moment she walked out and focused on her. She met his gaze and saw him staring back. His nostrils flared.

Shit. He wasn't a Vampire. It was still bright outside. He had a stocky build, sporting a fishing T-shirt and jeans. Her gaze lowered down his body as she returned to her seat, storing her packs on the floor. It was easy to fuss with her bags, purposely avoiding looking at his face again. He wore slip-on shoes. *Lycan.* She was sure of it.

He wasn't from her pack. He also wasn't from any of the nearby ones. She didn't recognize him. That was a bonus. Worst case, he got a whiff of her parents coming off her backpack and that she'd had sex with Creed. He wouldn't dare approach her around other people to appease his curiosity if he'd never been around a GarLycan. She adjusted her hair over her shoulder to hide the bandage.

"Sir?" the woman behind the counter called out.

Angel looked up and watched the Lycan coming right at her. She swallowed hard and sat back, masking her features as she looked directly into his eyes. He didn't stop until he stood right in front of her.

"Come with me."

"Excuse me?" She studied his face. It wasn't good when she noticed that he seemed to have more hair on it than before. He cocked his head and sniffed at her again. The tip of one ear looked a little pointier than it should have. He was starting to shift, even if it was just a tiny bit.

"Now," he hissed.

Panic rose fast when she looked at the hand he held out to her. His nail beds were thicker and the tips of them pointy. The crazy bastard seemed ready to shift in front of a room full of humans if he didn't get control of himself. He would expose Lycans.

She ignored his hand and leaned forward, snatching her bags. "Okay, Mike. We can talk outside. You don't have to *make a scene.*" She stressed the words, hoping it would clue him in.

He looked down at his hand, shock spreading across his features. Then he spun, rushing with long strides toward the door. She followed him. They cleared the building and she trailed him to the side of it, away from the prying eyes of anyone from the airfield. He leaned against the wall and covered his face with his hands.

"Take deep breathes," she encouraged. "Are you okay? What's your real name?"

He peeked at her between his fingers. "You know?"

"That you were about to sprout fur in there? Yeah. I belong to the Henita pack. My alpha is Picoz."

"You're not one of my kind." He dropped his hands. "What are you?"

She locked her knees, remembering that she smelled like sex still, and Creed. "That's none of your business but I'm pack protected. I'm going back inside now, and you need to pull yourself together before you do."

He sniffed at her and groaned. "You smell so good!"

She backed up. "Thanks."

"Come here." He reached for her with both hands and growled.

She saw lust glitter in his eyes and his breathing increased almost to a pant. She knew the signs well. "Oh, hell no. Are you in heat? You crazy son of a bitch. Go into the woods and call someone from your pack to come get you. You can't be around humans in that condition. Are you suicidal?"

He lunged forward and grabbed her. She was spun and her back hit the wall hard. Her packs slipped down her arm and then he was up against her, pinning her. He buried his nose against her throat and groaned. He thrust the front of his jeans against her belly, rubbing hard, almost humping her.

Angel used her free hand to shove against his chest but he wouldn't budge. He had a hundred pounds on her but he wasn't much taller. She shook her other arm, dropping her packs. It gave her the ability to get a good hold on the belt he wore. She twisted her head a little, looking around. No one was within sight, thankfully.

130

"I'm going to fuck you so good," he snarled.

Angel braced one foot against the wall and bucked her hips at him with all her strength, shoving him enough to make him stumble.

She struck fast when she got a little space between them, slamming her fist into his groin. It was a direct hit and she twisted her body, kicking him in the knee. He crumpled to the ground and she went for his hair, grabbing a handful of it and stepping around him.

"Knock your shit off," she demanded. "Don't make me hurt you. You're in heat and you've lost your mind. What was the plan? Fuck me right here against the wall so we could just wave to anyone who passed? Get control!"

He snarled and tried to twist his head. He snapped at her wrist with his mouth but she jerked away fast. He sported full-on fangs and facial hair now. His nose had bowed out a little into a mini snout. It pissed her off that he'd attempted to take a bite out of her.

She punched him for all she was worth, slamming her fist into his jaw. "Control," she snapped.

He collapsed onto his ass but recovered fast. Wolf eyes glared at her. "Mine!"

She frantically looked around as he got to his feet. No people had shown up yet but it was only a matter of time. The airport was small but there was steady light traffic. She dodged him when he tried to grab her around her waist and threw out her elbow, catching him in the ribs. He grunted and stumbled past her. She twisted, sending a roundhouse kick that nailed him in the ass. He plowed face first into the ground.

The damn Lycan had lost his mind. She sprinted to her backpacks, caught the straps in her hand, and ran to the back of the building. A large plane hangar caught her attention. She fled toward it to find cover. One door had been left open but she didn't see anyone inside. She heard the Lycan coming after her. He snarled as if he had rabies or something. She ran inside with him following her.

She tossed the packs out of the way and turned. He spotted her and snarled louder. Hair covered his arms now, so matted she couldn't even see skin. The idiot probably had a tail smashed inside his jeans too at that point. He grabbed the front of his shirt and tore it open. Hair covered him from shoulders to waist.

"Mine!"

He didn't just want to fuck her. He planned on claiming her. She wasn't sure what pack he'd been raised in but it wasn't one like hers. The men courted their women first, got permission, but never forced a mating. It was obvious he didn't plan to ask. He tossed the destroyed shirt aside and kicked off his shoes.

"No. Do you hear me? No! I already have a mate."

He snarled and stalked closer, his arms opening.

"Did you hear me? I'm already taken."

He lunged, claws out. She ducked but he managed to catch a few of her hairs with his sharp tips. It wasn't pleasant, having them ripped out. She threw another kick, nailing him in the back of his thighs that time. He went down but just twisted on his hands and knees. He crouched there.

She was in a lot of trouble. He wasn't listening to her. She backed up and almost tripped on a toolbox that some pilot or mechanic had left out. She swiftly grabbed a long-handled wrench.

"Don't make me hurt you," she warned.

"Come here." He pointed a clawed tip at the floor directly in front of him.

"It's so not going to happen. I'm not going to shove down my jeans and assume the position. I'm not the submissive type. Did you hear what I said? I'm *already taken*."

"By me!" He sprang up, diving at her.

She held still, her heart hammering until he was almost on top of her. At the last second, she threw her body to the right, rolling on the unforgiving floor and getting to her feet.

The Lycan landed on the toolbox and crashed into the wall. It was loud and she prayed no one would come investigate.

She didn't give him time to recover. She went at him and nailed him with the metal wrench to the back of his head, hoping it would knock him out. He was lifting up when the blow hit. It knocked him flat. The toolbox was on its side and some of the contents had spilled out. She saw a roll of duct tape and dropped onto his back.

She pegged him in the head a second time when he started to push up. Lycans had thick skulls. She didn't want to seriously hurt him, but she sure wasn't going to let him rip off her clothes and fuck her, either. He went still under her. She leaned over, trying to reach the tape. It was just out of reach. She bit her lip and stretched more, her fingers inching closer.

Someone stepped right next to it.

Angel stared at the big black set of boots—and froze. How was she supposed to explain to a human what was going on without them calling the state troopers? She had no clue.

Her chin lifted to stare at leather pants, and higher, to the man wearing them.

"Shit."

He *wasn't* human. He wore dark glasses over his eyes and his sheer size screamed enforcer. He had wide shoulders, arms a bodybuilder would turn green with envy over, and looked deadly. The half-sword strapped to his thigh was another hint. No human would have the balls to walk around with a weapon like that in civilian areas or they'd be arrested. He had probably been sent by his pack to track down the man she'd just been beating on. Packs tended to frown on that.

"I can explain," she got out, trying to keep calm. "Your guy here is in heat. Look at his back. He's all hair. I didn't want to hurt him but he didn't leave me much of a choice."

She moved real slow as she climbed off the limp body under her. She dropped the wrench. She opened her hands and raised them to show she didn't have a weapon anymore.

He said nothing. She couldn't see his eyes but felt his stare. It gave her chills—and not the good kind. She took a few steps backward to put space between them and his downed pack mate.

"I wasn't trying to kill him. That's why I was going for the tape. I just planned to tie him up and drag him somewhere he wouldn't be found by anyone working in the airport. I have a cell phone in my bag. I would have called it in. I didn't want a human to find him."

The scary stranger tilted his head and his lips twisted into a frown.

"For real. I'm really glad you showed up instead. That's why we're in here. He lost his control inside the airport. He couldn't be reasoned with."

The silence was awful.

Then something crunched near the door, and she turned her head to spot another enforcer guarding the entrance. He was just as big as the first one. They were almost dressed like twins except the second one wasn't wearing a half-sword. They even had similar features, both their hair jet black, cut short.

"He's not one of ours."

She looked back at the first one, who'd finally spoken. "Oh. Well, can you take him to your pack if you're local until he's fit for walking around again?"

"We're not pack."

Chapter Nine

Angel looked him over from head to foot. He wasn't human. She couldn't be that wrong, and his voice didn't sound it either. Only non-humans spoke that deep and gruff. It was still sunny outside. He also had tan skin. That left out Vampire, unless...

Her heart raced as the other alternative came to her.

"I've never met a VampLycan. I belong to a pack. I was raised with Lycans. We're cool. Can you take him somewhere safe at least? Nobody can see him. We both know that."

"You're not pack."

"I was adopted. I *am* pack. I know you're reading me as human. Guilty. But I'm still pack. You don't need to wipe my memories. I have a plane to catch. May I go now?"

"You're not getting on that plane."

Dread pitted in her stomach. VampLycans were law-keepers. Maybe they thought she had committed a crime. "I was sitting inside and he came right at me. He was about to shift so I hauled ass outside to make sure it didn't happen in front of all those passengers. I tried to talk some sense into him but he wouldn't listen. I had no choice but to knock him out. I swear!"

"We saw."

It took her a second to recover. "You did?"

He gave a sharp nod.

That pissed her off. "You didn't think to maybe help me? He wasn't messing around."

"I was curious how you'd handle yourself."

She really didn't like the guy. "And if I hadn't been able to? Would you have allowed him to hurt me?"

"No."

It didn't make her any less mad. "Gee, thanks. That's such a relief." She lowered her arms and retrieved her backpacks. "I'm out of here."

She turned away from him and walked toward the door. The second enforcer stepped into her path and shook his head.

She stopped. "Please move."

"No." He crossed his arms over his chest and spread his legs, making it clear she wasn't getting around him.

She wasn't sure what to do. There was no way she'd be able to fight her way out. She spun back to the first one. He had walked over to the downed Lycan and snapped on handcuffs. He lifted the man and threw him over his shoulder as easily as if he were a sack of laundry.

"You said you saw what happened. I didn't start this. I just did the smart thing by getting him away from the humans. I didn't break any laws. I also explained why I'm a human who knows about this stuff. You have no reason to detain me. I don't want to press charges. It's obvious the guy's in heat and lost his mind. It happens. It was stupid for him to leave his territory at this time but I'm sure the headache he's going to have when he wakes up will be punishment enough. No harm was done."

137

What she didn't say was she wouldn't want to stick around even if he *had* hurt her. It was time to leave, and she didn't want to miss her flight.

"You will come with us." He carried the Lycan closer and jerked his head toward the other enforcer. "Go with him. We have an SUV around the corner."

She didn't budge. "Under pack regulations, you have no right to arrest me. Don't make me call my alpha. I will."

"You're not pack and you don't have an alpha."

She really was beginning to hate this guy. He probably thought just because she was born human, it made her inferior enough to not have the right to be in a pack. "Listen. I *am* pack and my alpha will tell you that. I'm going to get my cell phone out and you can speak to him. Not everyone is a thick-skulled, prejudiced asshole like you."

"I like her," the second enforcer muttered. "You *can* be a bit of an asshole, Chaz."

She turned her head, wishing she could see his eyes. The sunglasses they wore were too dark though. "Thank you."

"He's not in charge," Chaz stated. "I am."

She looked back at him.

"I'm not saying you aren't pack because you're human." He stepped closer. "We're also not VampLycans. We're GarLycans. Creed mated you—and that makes you one of ours. Now turn your ass around and follow my brother Fray to the SUV. You're in enough deep shit as it is, Angel."

"I'm so fucked," she muttered.

138

Fray grunted. "I wouldn't mention anything with the word 'fuck' in it right now. Chaz and I aren't mated. Didn't you think it was strange that this Lycan would come after you and go almost feral? You smell like a bitch in heat, amplified by about ten. You fried the poor bastard's brain. Be happy we're able to control our urges more so than Lycans. But my dick is hard, and I'm betting Chaz's is too. It's why we just watched you fight instead of grabbing you to get you out of the way. You don't want either of us getting too close to you right now. Understand?"

His words left her speechless.

"It's a GarLycan new-mate thing," Chaz added. "Creed didn't know. Just walk, and try not to bump up against either of us. We're taking you to your mate. He's hopefully going to meet us soon. I don't know how long I can take being around you."

"You don't do humans," Fray stated.

"I might if I find one like her. You have to admit, even holding our breaths, her fighting skills made her hot."

"So fucking hot." The one named Fray grinned. "It's a shame you're already mated, Angel. I'd toss you over my shoulder otherwise and we'd both find heaven together."

"Let's go," Chaz sighed. "Stop flirting, Fray. Move, Angel. Don't run."

Angel had to admit she was tempted to make a run for it, but they'd said they were taking her to Creed. Clearly his people were already aware of what they'd done. She nodded. "I'll go with you."

There was a black SUV parked on the other side of the small terminal. Chaz opened the back and dumped the Lycan inside. She noticed both men kept at least four feet from her. He pointed to the front.

139

"Take the passenger seat. Fray can drive. I'm going to sit in the back in case this guy wakes up and tries to get at you again. We'll drop him off a few miles out in the woods and I'll take off the cuffs. He'll be able to walk back when he's fit for that."

She placed her backpacks on the floorboards at her feet and put on her belt. She noticed Fray didn't bother as he climbed into the driver's seat. He started the engine, kicked up the air conditioning, and pushed buttons to make all the windows go down.

"It's going to get cold for you in here but it will stop you from sweating as much. Sorry."

Fray seemed nicer than his brother, so she questioned him. "Is Creed okay?"

"I'd be worried about your own ass."

She crossed her arms over her chest. "It was all my fault. I want to officially state that. Creed shouldn't be punished. I pushed him into mating me."

He turned his head as he pulled away from the side of the building. "Are you sure you want to say that?"

"Yes."

"You forced Creed into it, huh?"

"I did."

He watched the road. "Last time I saw Creed, he was a bit bigger than you."

"I was raised as a Lycan. I'm way tougher than I look."

He grinned. "Did he try to chain you down, and you fought him off until he snapped?"

She sealed her lips.

"Damn. I was kidding." Fray's voice deepened. "Did he force you?"

"No!"

He turned his head and seemed to study her before he had to watch the road again. "You volunteered for his ravage?"

"Yes."

"Did you change your mind at the last minute or something when you realized he had to chain you? Then put up a fight?"

She shook her head, staring out the window. "That's not what happened. It's complicated but it's my fault."

"I'll call Kelzeb and tell him we have her." Chaz sighed loudly from the back.

"Can you call Creed?" She twisted in the seat to look at Chaz.

"He's with Kelzeb. He'll know."

"Can I talk to him?"

"No."

"But—"

"No," Chaz repeated. "It's bad enough we were pulled off our assignment to go pick up a wayward mate before she got herself killed...or someone else. Just sit back and shut up."

"You really are an asshole," she muttered.

"He is," Fray agreed. "Pity me. I've had to deal with him since conception." He glanced back. "I should have punched you in the womb to make my exit first. Then you'd have been born second."

"Shut up," Chaz snorted.

She closed her eyes and relaxed in the seat while she could. She'd see Creed soon and they'd be taken to his Lord Aveoth. It seemed like things were going to get a lot worse.

* * * * *

Creed couldn't relax. All he could think about was how Angel had been attacked by a Lycan, and now two GarLycans were enclosed inside a vehicle with her while she was putting out the calling.

What if they can't resist and start fighting over her? What if...

Kelzeb cleared his throat. "They aren't going to do anything to her. They're twin brothers and they are very close to each other. One isn't going to take out the other. She's safe."

It didn't help. "How much longer?"

"Soon. Don't annoy me. You've asked that four times already."

Creed wiped his palms on his jean-clad thighs. He shouldn't have listened to Angel and her plans. She could be irrational. He knew that. She had a free spirit and took that into her thought process.

"Don't shut down, either."

"I'm just thinking," Creed admitted.

"Damn, I hope I don't find my mate for centuries more. It turns intelligent men into lunatics."

"I really didn't know she'd suffer the calling."

"Remind me to get you a copy of that video I made of our dads getting their asses verbally handed to them by Aveoth when you have your mate safely at your side, and before you see your father. You might really kill him otherwise."

"He hates humans."

"You rescued one. Was he aware that you had feelings for her?"

Creed shook his head. "I told my mother everything. She worried I had become antisocial after my assignments. I admitted that I spent time with Angel. It was before she said that she wanted to be my mate though."

"What did your mother say about a human wanting to spend her life with you?"

"I never had the chance to ask. My mother died a week after Angel brought up becoming my mate. It was a conversation I planned to have with my mother face to face instead of over the phone."

"Your father probably worried you'd consider a human for a mate after you saved one. It implied you didn't hate them or believe they were beneath your notice. You know how full-bloods are about that. He wouldn't have wanted you to form an attachment of some sort to the girl. And she was part of the pack you protect; even I could guess she might be the one to volunteer to help you during your time of need. They don't call it the ravage for nothing. Look at what full-blood bastards did in the past."

"I never heard why it was called that."

Kelzeb hesitated. "Our forefathers were vicious. We've always had the issue of birthing more boys than girls. The desire to breed would come upon them and they'd hunt for a woman. They preferred Gargoyle ones but you know their birthrate is low. So they'd kidnap humans and take them to their lairs. No one volunteered for that. It was pretty violent. Those women would be chained and taken against their will. You're young, so you don't know how humans used to be. They would go insane after being exposed to one of us. Imagine being forced to drink something that made you actually want to have sex with your kidnapper who looked like a demon. Their lives were destroyed regardless of the outcome."

"Outcome?"

"The ones who got pregnant were kept chained and locked inside the Gargoyle's lair until they birthed for him. He couldn't risk her throwing herself off the ledge before she delivered the child. It happened sometimes. The ones who were released afterward were usually murdered when they told their people what happened to them. Their families and neighbors believed they were exposed to evil, and it was safest to kill the women to keep the devil from coming back.

"It was named the ravage because any woman was destroyed if she was chosen to be a breeding vessel. Take your pick on what was worse. Being forced to birth a child for who they thought was the devil, or being killed by their own families and friends after being freed."

"I'm glad we ask for volunteers now. I could never do that to a woman."

"No shit. I've gone through the ravage, and it's hell, but I would chain myself to a wall before I forced a woman into my bed. I would never be able to forgive myself."

"Nor would I," Creed agreed. "I've only experienced it twice but I'd have chained myself too if the women hadn't been willing."

"What was your first one like?"

He hesitated. "Cold."

"How in the hell can you say that?"

"My father arranged it. It was with Winalin. He had an understanding with her brother. They wanted us to breed. I'd planned to unchain her and tell her to run away. I didn't want to have a youngling that my father would take possession of. Winalin and I spoke once they put us together in guest quarters, and she wasn't happy with the arrangement either. Unfortunately, they had locked us in and we were stuck together."

Kelzeb shot him a horrified look but said nothing.

"We both felt resentment, being ordered to be together by our family members. The sex was pleasurable but it was nothing like with Angel. There is no comparison."

"Because you have feelings for Angel."

"It's more than that. She's very passionate."

"Wasn't Winalin?"

"No. She refused to drink my hormones for fear of being unable to prevent ovulation in her body. Neither of us wanted her pregnant. I mostly feared harming her, since she wasn't as turned on as I was."

"That does sound cold. We've reached the meeting point; they're waiting."

Creed sat up straighter, staring at the SUV parked on the side of the road. The Jeep had barely come to a stop when he'd shoved open the door and rushed forward. The scent of Angel almost took him to his knees. She opened the passenger door and he grabbed her around her middle, lifting her right off her feet.

He studied her face, throat, and arms with a quick glance. "Were you hurt?"

She gripped his shoulders. "I'm fine."

"I heard you were attacked by a Lycan."

"I'm okay."

He pulled her closer, hugging her. His dick had become rock hard. His Angel smelled like pure sex. It made him want to rip off her clothes and take her right against the black vehicle. He was only able to resist because three GarLycans were in close proximity to his mate. His protective instincts were keeping his lust in check. Barely.

The two doors on the other side of the SUV opened and the twin enforcers climbed out.

Creed backed up with Angel in his arms. His body fluxed a little when his skin tightened, trying to shell to make him tougher to kill. Both men were reading as a danger to his mate, despite the fact that they'd brought her to him. It was difficult to reason with his mind with Angel in his arms.

"Creed." Kelzeb used a soft tone. "Don't. She's in no danger. We are expected by Lord Aveoth. No one is going to touch her. Control your body now. Anyone could drive by and see you. That's an order."

He closed his eyes and slowed his breathing. Angel was with him and safe. He got a leash on his lust and instincts. It wasn't easy, but he'd had sixty years to learn discipline. His skin stopped tingling and he lowered Angel to her feet. He opened his eyes and met Kelzeb's stare. "I'm fine now."

The other man sighed. "Good. Keep it that way. You and your mate ride with me." He glanced at Fray and Chaz. "You two follow. We're going home. The talks with the packs have been rescheduled."

"Fantastic," Chaz muttered. "I fucking hate them anyway."

Fray chuckled. "Only because the women avoid us two and flirt with the others. We scare them with our eyes."

"I don't want a mate," Chaz growled.

"Sure you don't." His twin snorted.

Chapter Ten

Angel wasn't certain what to expect of the place Creed called home when he wasn't living in his cave perched high above her village. She'd never seen another GarLycan until that airport hangar, and then the third one who'd arrived with Creed to meet her alongside the road.

So far, her impression of his people didn't bode well for her future.

All three men were a bit intimidating. They showed no emotion when they climbed out of their vehicles in an out-of-the-way spot off a dirt road. She stood in official GarLycan territory. They'd passed an electronic security gate that had closed off the road a mile before they'd parked.

Kelzeb addressed Creed, not sparing her a glance. "I'll take her up. She needs to be presentable before meeting with Lord Aveoth. You need to change clothes."

Creed stepped in front of her, putting his body between Angel and the enforcer. "I'll fly her to my lair and see to it."

"No." Kelzeb softened his voice. "She'll be taken to Galihia. You know the rules. She'll be safe. I give you my word. You wouldn't have anything appropriate for her to wear. You're already in deep shit. Do you want to make things worse? Don't fight me, Creed. The last thing you need is to appear in court wearing chains."

Angel could feel the tension and she reached out, placing her hand on Creed's broad back. "It's okay."

He turned his head, staring down at her. His eyes had gone black. She was starting to guess they did that when he was angry or his emotions were in serious turmoil.

"It's okay," she repeated. It horrified her to think of him being put in chains. She even managed to force a smile to hide her uneasiness. "I'll be fine."

He said nothing, just stared down at her.

"Don't get into more trouble over me," she whispered. "Please?"

That seemed to sway him. "Do everything you are told." He turned and reached up, grabbing a thick lock of her hair with his fingers. "Rein in your attitude for me. I find it amusing but they won't. Do you understand?"

It was a clear warning. "I'll be on my best behavior."

"Treat everyone as if you are in the presence of a visiting elder."

In other words, his people were formal and would take any lip as a sign of great disrespect. "I understand."

"It's important, Angel. It would be bad otherwise."

She wanted to hug him but refrained. Her fear notched a little higher but she tried to hide it from him. She had no idea what the laws of his people were with regards to etiquette or how harsh their reprimands would be, but his grim tone implied a lot. It would be really severe. She nodded.

"You won't like the clothing but don't refuse." He paused. "Try not to speak at all unless they ask you a direct question."

She really wanted him to explain more but Kelzeb cleared his throat.

"The scouts would have notified Lord Aveoth that we've arrived. Making him wait will irritate him. We need to go."

Creed took a step back from her and nodded. "How long until I'm expected in court?"

"Give it an hour. I want to speak to him first." Kelzeb removed his shirt and tossed it inside his Jeep. He slowly approached. "I'm going to take her. Leash yourself."

Creed grew totally still. "Do it."

The big GarLycan stepped behind Angel. One of his arms looped her hips, the other locked around her just above her breasts. He pulled her tight against his body and she didn't protest. He lowered his head a little. "Just be still. I won't drop you."

That's all the warning he gave. He lifted her off her feet, bent his knees a little, and then jumped. His wings thumped hard, taking them into the sky.

She grabbed at his arms just for something to cling to. Creed had never flown with her that way. He cradled her in his arms but this GarLycan just kept her locked in front of him. It was more frightening, knowing she could plummet to her death if she slipped from his hold as they rose higher, the ground getting farther way.

He banked to the right sharply, and she gasped and drew her knees up.

"You won't fall."

They flew between a pair of mountains. There were woods as far as the eye could see, with no signs of houses or roads below. She twisted her head, staring behind them. Three figures were back there, one of them Creed. It made her feel a little better, knowing he remained close. He'd catch her if Kelzeb dropped her. She'd seen how fast he could move when he dove as he flew.

"Your mate is on the edge. Don't scream," Kelzeb warned. "He'd attack me in flight. That would mean you might slip from my hold. Am I clear?"

"Yes." She wasn't liking him much at that moment.

"We're almost there."

"Couldn't we just drive?"

"We purposely make it very difficult for anyone to reach our cliffs by foot or vehicle. There is very rough terrain, and we bring in a lot of territorial animals to help us defend the land against intruders."

They cleared the two mountains and turned left. That's when she first spotted the cliffs. It was a massive mountain with a sheer side. It split in a few places, showing off some vegetation where trees had grown, but most of it was a flat face of sharp-looking rock. She looked up, realizing it extended high into the air.

"That's it?"

"Yes. Let me give you some advice."

She turned her head, looking up at him. "What?"

"Do everything Galihia says. She's Lord Aveoth's mother. She's a GarLycan with a heart, so her advice will be given in your best interest. Listen to her."

"Thank you."

He flew them higher. She examined the area of cliff they flew toward. It surprised her when she saw a bunch of open ledges and openings. "How many people live here?"

"Dozens. We live a little spaced apart for privacy. Stay away from the ledges. You wouldn't survive if you slipped. I hope you're not afraid of being inside caves, because this might be the last time you're allowed outside for a while."

He banked his wings and they dropped. It made Angel feel a little sick. Then he landed, and it knocked the air out of her lungs, but she wasn't hurt. She turned her head, searching for any sign of Creed. Kelzeb blocked her view though when he marched her forward into a dark hole in the cliff.

She couldn't see anything until he turned. Faint lights showed that she was inside a tunnel. It wasn't like anything she'd ever seen before. The rock walls had been smoothed until they were nicely shaped. He stopped and lowered her to her feet.

"Stay at my side."

"As if I want to get lost. Not."

He shook his head. "That's the kind of talk you don't want to do here. Just agree. Our women were born in another time. Do you understand?"

"No."

He blew out his breath. "My mother is two hundred and twenty-six years old. I would guess that Galihia is about a hundred and twenty, give or take some years. They are from a time when women were more submissive to men. A lot of them never leave the cliffs. No man wants his mate at risk. Just be quiet and try to learn our ways. Watch every word you say. Creed and I are considered young, but so is anyone under a hundred. We've also spent a lot of our lives away from here. We're more modern. Most of the people here aren't. Is that clear enough?"

"Yes."

"You shouldn't stare into a man's eyes when you're speaking to them. Dip your chin and only give them glances if they speak directly to you."

"Are you serious?"

"Yes."

She sighed and dropped her gaze to stare at his chest. He had a nice one, but it still felt weird. "Like this?"

"Yes."

"I feel rude since you're not wearing a shirt. I'm not checking you out."

He barked out a harsh laugh. "It's only appropriate to be without a shirt when we've just flown in."

"Creed wears those thin-strapped tank tops. He can get his wings out in them without a problem."

"It would be ruder to wear them here than to just be bare. They would be considered indecent by our standards. Let me take you to Galihia. Be very polite and respectful to her."

"I will be."

He gripped her arm. "This way." He led her forward.

A big guy approached from the other direction. She tried not to stare. He wore leather pants, military-style boots, and a thin black material stretched tight over his muscled upper body. His eyes were a dark green with enough silver that they seemed to nearly glow. The sword strapped to his hip was scary looking, especially when he reached for it, wrapping his hand around the handle.

Kelzeb jerked Angel by her arm, shoving her behind him. "Stand down."

"Who is she?"

"A new mate."

"Who does she belong to? You?"

Kelzeb deepened his voice and it echoed when he spoke. "Keep walking. You're not challenging for her."

"Who does she belong to?"

"Not you. Her and her mate have an audience with Lord Aveoth."

Angel peeked around Kelzeb's broad back. The other guy still gripped his sword handle but his eye color had faded a little so they weren't so silver. He locked them on her.

"Who do you belong to?"

"Don't answer that," Kelzeb snapped.

He reached back with his other arm and shifted her to his other side, still keeping her behind him. His hold was almost painful as he stepped forward, taking her with him. They walked past the other man. He didn't attack but as soon as they were away from the stranger, Kelzeb yanked her in front of him so he kept his body between her and the other guy. They turned a corner.

"What was that about?"

"You are giving off the calling. Any unmated man in here is going to investigate and consider challenging for you. Your mating bond is weak and not fully formed yet."

"What does that mean?"

"They might be tempted to fight Creed to the death. He isn't well known here and has few friends. It means more than likely they'll challenge to take his mate. You don't want that. He's a skilled fighter but some of these men are on the battlefield often. Creed isn't. He could be rusty with his sword."

That made her afraid for Creed. "What do you guys fight here?"

"Vampires mostly, from the larger cities if they're getting out of hand. We fly in and take out some of their numbers. Occasionally we'll get Gargoyles flying in from Europe when they believe they can invade our territory. We're not far from Russia, they also come at us from that way. Full-bloods are pretty fierce."

"You guys invade each other's territories? Why?"

"You're from a Lycan pack. Why do others invade your territory?"

"They want to take over when they've expanded their numbers to the point that they need land to add to their territory. Sometimes it's to gain access to more women."

"Exactly." He kept her moving. They reached the top of stone stairs and he led her down, keeping a firm hold on her arm.

"How big is this place?"

He seemed to debate answering her, or maybe how to answer. She almost gave up on expecting him to say anything when he finally spoke.

"Are you familiar with an ant farm?"

"Yes."

"Think of the interior of these cliffs like one of those. All the homes are linked internally, but we all have exterior entrances that can be sealed off if we're attacked or in harsh weather. All of our community areas are deep inside, so they're protected."

"Have you ever had a full-on attack happen?"

"No, but we are prepared for that event."

They came to the bottom of the steps and another interior corridor. Lights were along the walls about every twenty feet. She got a good look at them. "Electricity?"

"Generators. We *have* modernized somewhat."

"Solar or gas?"

"Why do you ask?"

"I'm curious."

"We have a river that runs through the base of our mountain. We use the flow of water to create power for our generators. Everything is self-contained from the outside world."

"That's impressive. What about when the winter comes and the water freezes?"

"We can switch to fuel but the water runs so deep that it never completely freezes. We're a very old race. Now stop with your questions." He halted in front of a massive wooden door. "We're here. Be respectful. Lord Aveoth is more powerful than your alpha, and this is his mother."

Angel nodded. "I understand."

He shot her a grim look. "I hope so." He raised a fist and pounded on the door.

The door opened quickly—and Angel tried not to gawk.

The woman was tall and very pretty. Long black hair had been neatly coiled around the crown of her head, then looped into a twisted rope that fell to her waist. Angel figured if it were real, the woman's hair probably trailed behind her as she walked if it were ever set free of the elaborate hairstyle. The GarLycan leader's mother was also rail thin and sporting a gown that looked right out of a ballroom.

"Lady Galihia." Kelzeb released Angel and bowed deeply at his waist. "I present Angel. She is Creed's mate." He straightened. "I hope you were informed of her arrival. I apologize for my state of undress."

"It's fine. I was expecting her. Thank you." She opened the door more. "Enter, Angel."

She glanced at Kelzeb. He jerked his head, indicating she should go. She walked into the room and stopped short, openly staring around. It was as if she'd stepped back in time. It looked nothing like a cave. The dark wood floors, the loaded bookshelves lining one wall, and the big fireplace gave it an elegant library look. Fancy couches and a few tables were the only furniture. A painting hung over the mantel of the woman before her, holding an infant in her arms.

The door closed behind her and she forced her attention back on Lady Galihia. She didn't even appear to be thirty in human years but that didn't come as a surprise to Angel.

"How do you do?" It was the politest thing she could think to say; she'd heard it a movie.

"I am well. How are you, child?"

"It's been a strange day."

"I imagine so. Please follow me. A bath awaits you." Galihia glanced down Angel's body. "I'll send for Renna. She'll make certain you have a gown."

Angel followed the woman down a wood-paneled hallway past closed doors to the one at the end. Lady Galihia opened it, revealing a massive bedroom. There were no windows anywhere but the interior looked as if they were in a real house, one that was a few hundred years old but with electricity. There were tall ceilings and even a chandelier hanging in the center. An open archway let her see a claw-foot bathtub.

"My bed chamber." She walked over to a corded rope and tugged on it. "I have called for Renna. This must be bizarre for you. Do you have any questions?"

"How does pulling on that cord get someone to come?"

"It runs all the way to the ceiling, where there's a rope that rings a bell at the other end of it in Renna's chambers next door. She'll hurry to see what I need. She's my aunt and attendant."

"What's that?"

Lady Galihia chuckled. "She looks after me. You'll like her. She's a Lycan. I was told you were raised as one but you're fully human."

"I am."

"How did a human come to be with them?"

"Creed saved me when I was a child."

"How did he do that?"

"I don't remember much about my before life. That's what we call it. There are bits and pieces. My biological father yelled all the time and I remember being afraid of him. He had a girlfriend. She was worse. They hit me a lot. Creed took me from them and gave me to my parents. It makes my mom cry when we talk about it. I guess I was in really bad shape that night. I'd been beaten and had sores from neglect. I was also skinny and underfed. They adopted me and gave me a great life." She hesitated. "I probably wouldn't have survived where I'd been. My dad told me that he got the impression from something Creed said that I was about to be murdered when he rescued me."

"And now he's your mate."

"He's always been kind of a hero to me," she admitted. "I didn't notice how handsome he was until I was much older, when he started coming around. I almost thought I'd dreamed him from the night he'd rescued me as a child, until I saw him again."

"Didn't he protect your pack?"

"He only came down to talk to the elders at night, and that was way past my bedtime when I was young. We all heard about the guardian as kids but never saw him. He was almost like a myth or something." She smiled. "Then one day he came to me during the daytime. I was sixteen and had almost walked into a bad situation with a bear and her cubs. Creed landed, put his hand over my mouth, and pointed out what I hadn't seen. He offered me his hand then and led me back to my village."

"You felt bound by honor to agree to be his mate."

"No." Angel shook her head. "I fell in love with him and threw myself at him right after I turned eighteen. He told me it couldn't be that way

159

between us and stopped seeing me. I actually moved away so it would hurt less. It was just too hard being that close to his lair, knowing he was up there, but he wouldn't talk to me anymore."

Lady Galihia's features softened. "How did you become his mate then?"

"My mom called me in Seattle and told me I needed to come home. I figured it had to be pretty important, since she'd never done that before. I got on the first available plane heading that way. She explained Creed was going into the ravage, and what that meant. No one in our village had volunteered to be with him, so I did."

"You owed him a debt for the life he'd given you, so you couldn't say no. You felt honor bound to offer your body to him. That's admirable."

"Actually, I was pretty mad. I wasn't going to do it. He'd rejected me once so I didn't think he was attracted to me. I was so upset that my mom thought I'd offer to go to bed with him that I went outside to cool down. Creed thought I was a lost hiker and flew down to scare me off, but then realized who I was. Do you really want to hear this?"

"I do."

"I saw him...and man, he was still as hot as ever." She inwardly winced. "Sorry. He was as attractive as ever."

Lady Galihia shook her head. "Please continue. Don't hold back. I enjoy how you speak. It's refreshing."

"Okay." Angel relaxed. "I guess the ravage had already begun, because he wasn't as reserved as he normally is. Who could resist that? I couldn't. He was showing feelings and he got turned on when I touched him."

160

"*You* made first physical contact?"

"You bet. I mean…yes. Who wouldn't? You have no idea how much I love him, and I've always wanted to be with him. I told him I was going to volunteer and he kind of freaked out. Then I made it clear that I wasn't taking no for an answer. I didn't leave him a choice."

Galihia expression became animated as she grinned. "How did you leave him with no choice?"

"I got in his face and wouldn't let go of him."

"So you're physically aggressive."

"You could say that."

A door opened across the room and an older Lycan woman entered. She wore a gown too. She paused, staring back at Angel. "This is her, Gali?"

"Yes. She's sharing a very entertaining story. She pursued Creed for the ravage."

The Lycan came forward, grinning. "Tell us more."

Angel glanced between them. They looked a bit too happy, and it made her nervous. "I'm not going to get him into trouble, am I? It was all my fault."

"No," Galihia answered. "We're intrigued. You see, in our culture, women do not pursue men."

"*Your* culture," Renna chuckled. "I chased your uncle. He didn't know what hit him. I was in heat and just stripped down in front of him when I found him alone. I ordered him to take me. He did. No hot-blooded man could withstand that."

161

Angel glanced between them again. "You're more than family. You're best friends," she guessed.

"Yes. My father was a Gargoyle who mated with a Lycan. My aunt came to me after her mate died." Lady Galihia's eyes glistened with tears. "I was so grateful she did."

"Hush now, Gali," the other woman murmured. "That is what family is for." Renna held Angel's stare. "It can be a bit cold around here. These people don't hug or touch unless sex is involved, and there's not much of that, either. They choose every word they speak with care. It's nice to be able to relax and just be. Gali here was mated to a Gargoyle. I got a case of the chills just being in the same room as him. I can't imagine being summoned to his bed chambers. You call me Renna, and this is Gali. We're not formal." She winked.

"He was very set in his ways," Gali agreed. "Now he's gone and I'm unmated."

"And better off," Renna muttered. "You need a nice Lycan in your life. He'd warm you right up."

"No. I couldn't ever leave here. Aveoth needs me."

"Your son is fine, and we love that dear Jill. She's good for him. So much personality and fire."

"Yes." Gali smiled. "She's lovely. My son needed her. I worried my mate had crushed his soul." She motioned toward the bathroom. "Let's get you in the bath, Angel. My son wants to see you. Don't allow him to frighten you. He isn't unkind."

162

"She's shorter than I thought she'd be but I'll find something appropriate for court to fit her." Renna brushed her hands over her own dress. "This is the worst thing about living here. These formal getups."

Angel glanced at the gowns. "They *are* pretty."

"They're also bulky," Renna sighed. "It's how they dress. The men here like to keep us covered from throat to toe. A little flash of cleavage is acceptable but nothing else. It helps them avoid feeling lusty. Jill is working on Aveoth to change our dress code to something more casual. Pants are never allowed in public on women. Now, tell us about your Creed."

"We're mostly interested in your physical aggression, and how he reacted to it."

"I don't know if you want to hear that, Lady Galihia," Angel admitted. "I was told to talk as little as possible by both Creed and Kelzeb."

"You heard Renna. Call me Gali. And of course they said that. They are worried you'll be a bad influence on us. Come. Remove your clothing and get into the bath. I hope you're comfortable with us present. You were raised Lycan."

Angel got a better look at the tub when they crossed the threshold into the other room. It was filled with a white liquid. "What is that?"

"It's a mixture of tree sap, goat's milk, and water. I know it looks a bit odd but it will mask your scent. It's warm."

Angel had no words.

"Continue about your Creed. How did the mating happen? Did he take your body before he could chain you?" Renna sounded a little excited. "I think that would be romantic."

"He wouldn't have," Gali disagreed. "I would guess he worried about being overly powerful for her body to withstand and became too cautious to begin. He lost his patience, and then was riddled with guilt for his brutal treatment."

"That's not how it went down." Angel started to undress. She wasn't thrilled to have to get into that bath but at least it didn't stink. "He chained me. It was the morning after, when he let me go, that I kind of messed things up."

"How?" Renna took her discarded clothes.

"He wanted to take me home but he was still showing signs of the ravage. I just wanted to touch him, so I did. He kept telling me to stop but I wouldn't listen. It's totally my fault. I seduced him."

"How romantic!" Renna giggled.

Angel tested the bath. The water was warm and a bit thick, like sitting in milk. She ran her fingers through it, looking at her palm. "Please tell me that I don't have to wash my hair in this."

"Your hair is fine." Gali leaned over and carefully gathered it all, holding it up. "How do you feel about being mated to Creed?"

She didn't have to think about it as she lowered and sank into the tub. "I love him. I wish he wasn't in trouble. I'm afraid for him."

"Think of yourself," Renna suggested. "It's the women who pay the highest prices in this culture when mates have broken any rules or laws. They use us as leverage against the men."

"Aveoth won't do that." Gali's tone cooled. "He would never kill a mate. He has his own. He'd want to fall if he lost his Jill."

"That's true." Renna put pins in Angel's hair to keep it in place so it wouldn't fall into the water.

Both women grew quiet and Angel closed her eyes after settling down into the tub. That was her biggest fear. What if Lord Aveoth did something that made Creed end his life so she'd be spared?

She fought the urge to cry. It wasn't going to happen. She wouldn't allow it.

Chapter Eleven

Angel hated the formal gown. Her middle was squeezed together so tight she could barely take a breath. Renna had put her in a corset. They were torture devices with laces along the back. Her breasts were probably permanently crushed in an upright position.

She couldn't even see her feet with the yards of material that made up the skirt, not that she planned on doing much bending, with her waist and chest locked into the corset. There wasn't a hoop that flared the skirt out, at least. She tried to be comforted by that. The gown covered everything except her hands and a small V of skin on her chest from the neck down.

The big man who escorted her to Lord Aveoth hadn't said a word. He opened a door and stood there. She hesitated and entered, hoping that's what he wanted, since he sure didn't give any hints.

The room was large and had an open balcony. She could see sky and the fresh air was nice to breathe. That was, until the man standing in the center of the room drew her attention.

Lord Aveoth was a striking, yet daunting figure. His good looks would make any woman feel at a loss for words and have a difficult time summoning thoughts.

"Come closer," he ordered.

She had a hard time taking those steps. Power seemed to radiate from him, and she knew a deadly predator when she saw one. He was lethal. She swallowed hard and tried to remember Gali's and Renna's advice. She stopped about six feet from him and bowed her head, lowering her gaze to the floor. Her knees bent in a curtsy before she straightened.

"Lord Aveoth." She was supposed to say it was a pleasure to meet him but couldn't do it. He scared her. She wanted to flee from the room.

"It was brought to my attention that Creed mated you. Did he explain why that shouldn't have happened?"

"Yes."

"You thought it was an acceptable risk and I'd have mercy?"

She wasn't supposed to look directly into his eyes, but his cold, angry tone didn't sit well with her. She raised her chin and met his glare. "No. It wasn't planned, and I take full responsibility."

He arched one eyebrow.

"It was my fault, Lord Aveoth."

"You overpowered Creed and forced him to mate you?" He swept his gaze over her from head to foot. "Did he ask you to say that?"

"No. He told me to let him take the blame.. But he was vulnerable and warned me to stop touching him. I actually just about tackled him to get him back on that bed. He demanded I stop but I didn't listen."

"He could have forced you away from him."

"Creed wouldn't risk hurting me. Have you been to his lair? It's all rock with just a thin rug carpet on the floor. There's only a bed and a small dresser in his bedroom. I would have either hit the floor or one of the walls if he'd thrown me off him. As a human, one blow to the head against rock could kill me. He'd never risk that. I straddled him and wasn't letting go. I did this. I didn't understand that he was fighting the urge to mate me."

"Why would you do that?"

"I just wanted to be with him one more time."

"You spent the night with him. That wasn't enough?"

"I was chained down and couldn't touch him all night. I knew it was a onetime thing, and I've loved him forever. I just wanted to do all the things I've fantasized about. It is my fault, Lord Aveoth. Creed shouldn't be punished for what I did." She sucked in air. "Do you feel anything?" She stepped closer. "I love him. I finally had the chance to be with him. He was going to take me home, and I'm human...I knew it was the only time I'd ever have with him. I just..." Her voice broke. "I wasn't willing to let him go yet. I wanted one more memory to take with me. It was going to have to last me until the day I died."

Aveoth frowned.

"I tried to get over how I felt about Creed. I couldn't stay with my pack, knowing he was so close but wouldn't spend time with me. I dated other men after I left home. It didn't work. I never got over Creed. I couldn't stop wishing he wanted me too. Then we were together finally, and I—"

"Enough."

She lowered her gaze. "Punish me instead. Please?" She looked at him again. "I think it's wrong that his father could promise a hundred years of his life to someone else, but I understand it's how your world runs. I respect that. Creed tried to keep me distanced. I threatened him. I told him I'd buy a grenade launcher and blow him out of his lair if he picked someone else to spend the night with during the ravage. I deserve to take whatever punishment you want to give him."

His features blanked. "I don't believe he took that threat seriously."

"You don't know me. You'd also be surprised at the kind of things you can buy on the internet. I meant it when I made that threat. The idea of him taking another woman up there probably would have driven me insane. I have a temper. He knows that. Please punish me instead."

"His punishment will be a hundred lashes and encasement for ten years."

"I know. He told me. I can't turn to stone but I'm sure you have cells here. We have them in my pack. I'll take the beating and the prison time. Just tell him you'll do it to me regardless of what he does. He threatened to fall to spare my life. He's a good man. I can't stand the idea of him being hurt because of me. I pushed him, Lord Aveoth. I refused to listen when he told me to stop, and he was emotional. I took advantage of knowing I could get away with it because I wanted to touch him."

"You're human. Do you know what it would mean if you were to agree to take his hundred lashes? We'd have to do it over a period of months so it wouldn't kill you. You'd have to heal and then take more." He paused. "It would leave you scarred and disfigured."

She inwardly winced. "I understand."

"Yet you are still willing to take his punishment?"

"Yes."

"Our cells have no light. You'd be in the dark."

"I figured. We're inside a mountain."

169

"Yet you still offer to take his punishment?"

"Yes."

He studied her. "Are you relying on me having mercy?"

"No. I was raised with a pack. I understand that it would cause opposition amongst your people. Lycans would challenge our alpha if they thought he was getting softhearted. They respect ruthlessness. Fear is needed to set boundaries, and those keep us safe as a whole. Every time a law is broken it could expose what we are to humans, and that puts everyone in danger. The punishment needs to be brutal enough to discourage others from even thinking about breaking a law again."

He grew quiet. She stood there waiting for him to tell her what he'd decided. She knew he was thinking about it. The urge to hug her waist was strong but she kept her hands down at her sides and even bowed her head, staring at the floor. Minutes dragged on.

"Creed has been in service to me since his birth sixty years ago. I reviewed his accomplishments. He was sent to patrol at a younger age than normal. He spent hardly any time here at the cliffs, beyond some of the training he received." He paused. "I was unaware of it, or I would have prevented him from being sent away at fifteen. It would have left him without the interaction he needed to fully mature the way the rest of our men do. It was also brought to my attention that he was sent somewhere on his first assignment that didn't allow for him to have access to women. He went through the first stage of manhood without temptations to learn to control his urges."

She glanced up, feeling hope. The callous look on Lord Aveoth's face dashed it. She fixed her gaze back on the floor.

"I've taken that into consideration, as well as what you've said. I have an understanding of humans, and you are one, despite the way you were raised. You're impulsive in your thinking and have no discipline when it comes to matters of the heart. I will not have Creed lashed and encased."

She could breathe easier.

"I also think it's distasteful to disfigure a woman, or kill one. We do value them, with our birthrate of females being so low. You are correct though. The laws must be followed, and punishment handed out when one is broken."

The silence that followed had her stomach in knots.

"I've threatened to spank my mate's bottom when she's being difficult. I would never actually do it because it would be painful for her." He sighed. "It won't disfigure you or cause you more than a week or two of discomfort. I sentence you to fifty strikes with a paddle and six months of confinement."

She was getting off easy. Her ass wouldn't think so, but out of all the things she'd expected, it was beyond merciful of Lord Aveoth. "Thank you."

"You don't wish to argue with me? Beg for a less-painful solution?"

She shook her head. "No. I'm grateful."

"You do understand that this is going to be painful? We aren't human. You'll be bruised and won't want to sit. One of my men will dole out your punishment."

She looked up at him then. "I'm keeping my head on my shoulders and Creed isn't going to endure any pain or prison time. That's all I care

171

about. Thank you. Six months is much better than ten years. I will count my blessings."

"Perhaps I was too lenient."

Horror struck.

He suddenly smiled. "It was a joke. I just wanted to see your reaction."

She didn't think it was funny but kept her mouth closed.

"I'll have you escorted to one of the chambers. I'll send a mated male to pass down my judgment, since it wouldn't be fair for you to remain in clothing. They'd cushion you somewhat from the pain. I apologize for any discomfort you'll suffer at being stripped, but it won't matter after the first few blows. You will be chained down. It will keep you from moving and keep him from accidently striking you anywhere that could do critical damage."

The guy had a way of putting things in perspective. He got points for that. "Thank you, Lord Aveoth."

"I do have one last question."

She looked up at him. "What?"

"Do you get into trouble often with your pack?"

"No."

"Thank you for answering with honesty. I spoke to your alpha. He told me you were always a well-behaved child. You may go."

She turned, almost making it to the door before he spoke again.

"Angel?"

She stopped and turned, holding his gaze. "Yes?"

"I'll be sure to tell Creed how you took the blame and asked to be the one punished."

"I wish you wouldn't. He'll be pissed."

He smiled. "I know. Go."

Her shoulders slumped, and she followed her escort down the hallway. They traveled somewhere lower in the mountain. *GarLycans keep in shape with the help of a lot of stairs*, she deduced by the time they finally reached a door, where he stopped. He opened it and gestured her inside. She hesitated but went in. There was no use putting it off or trying to drag it out.

It was a large bedroom with a massive bed. She saw the restraint setup and wondered if many of the rooms came with chains. The door closed and she turned, realizing that her guard remained. He crossed his arms over his chest.

"Strip bare and bend over the bottom of the bed. I'll restrain you and then guard the door until Lord Aveoth assigns someone to relieve me."

"Are you mated?"

"I am."

It was good enough for her. Mates didn't cheat. He wouldn't be interested in her as a woman. She wasn't wholly comfortable with getting naked in front of a stranger, especially a scary one, but things could be worse. She was still alive, and whoever came wouldn't be carrying a whip to tear open her skin.

She managed to remove all her clothing except the corset. She tried to twist to reach the ties but couldn't. It was impossible. Renna had put her in that contraption.

"Um…"

He sighed and approached her from behind. "Hold still."

He whipped out a dagger and just cut the lacing. She held the material over her breasts until he backed away. "Thanks."

"Assume the position. Do you need guidance?"

She dropped the corset and kept her back to him as she walked to the end of the bed. She bent, blushing. It was embarrassing. "No. I remember it well." She found a comfortable position lying flat on her stomach, after she went on her tiptoes so her hips were firmly curved against the soft padding. She stretched her arms straight out to the sides.

He walked around the bed and belted the restraint over one wrist, then rounded it to go to the other side. It was going to be worse if he chained her legs. One glance and he'd see more of her than she ever wanted him to. She didn't even know his name, and wasn't about to ask. He moved back when her arms were locked down.

"I'll be right outside the door." He reached into his pocket and withdrew a black handkerchief. "It will be easier for the man assigned to punish you if he doesn't see your tears. No one enjoys striking a woman." He bent and she closed her eyes before he tied it over her face. "Be strong for your mate. You are an extension of him."

She listened to his footsteps retreat. The door opened and then closed. She lay there waiting. The room was chilly but she welcomed the cold. It might numb her skin a little before she got her ass paddled. It wasn't going to be a swat on the butt from her parents. It was going to seriously hurt.

* * * * *

Creed entered the court chambers and bowed to Lord Aveoth. He glanced up, evaluating his leader's forbidding features. Cold emanated from the GarLycan's eyes and his body language displayed anger. It wasn't a good sign. Creed lowered to one knee, keeping his chin tucked.

"You couldn't wait forty years to take a mate?"

"It wasn't planned, Lord Aveoth."

"What would you like me to take into consideration?"

"Please have mercy on Angel. She's merely human. She didn't stand a chance against my strength and speed."

"You forced the issue?"

"She couldn't have fought me off."

"Do you regret it? Be honest."

"No. She isn't taking blood from her Lycan parents. She would have aged in human years."

"How old is she now?"

"Twenty-nine."

"I see the problem."

Creed glanced up, met Lord Aveoth's glare, then lowered his gaze. "All I ask is that you spare her."

"She won't age now. You'll do ten years encased and then be free to live with your mate. I can see how the punishment might have seemed worth committing the offense."

"It wasn't planned."

"You decided to mate her, rather than allow her to age until you weren't honor bound to me any longer?"

"I intended to speak to her parents and order them to give her blood, my lord."

"You felt you could overstep family bonds to issue that order? You wouldn't have been her mate if that was your plan."

"I gifted her to them. They tried to have children but couldn't. They owed me a debt. I never asked them for anything. I didn't believe they'd deny my one request."

"You follow the Lycans' lives so closely to know the status of every couple? How did you know this couple couldn't have children?"

He shook his head. "The female climbed part of my cliff. I thought she might wish to speak to me so I flew down to meet her. She never would have made it to my lair." He paused. "The rock is too steep. I feared she'd fall to her death in the attempt."

"And? What was so important?"

"She meant to free her mate. They'd tried to have children and she discovered the problem was with her body after seeing doctors. I talked her out of it. A mate is the one who stands by your side for life, but children leave the nest when they are grown. I felt certain she wasn't doing her mate a favor by releasing him to find another."

176

"She meant to fall?"

"Yes."

"And you searched for a child for them to raise?"

"No. It never crossed my mind, until I spotted a fire when I flew back to my post after coming here to meet with you. It had been reported that Vampires might be in that area so I wanted to take a closer look. I found a child being abused and a woman threatening to kill her. I believed it would happen. If not that night, another. I took her, knowing I could give her to a couple that would protect and love her."

"You felt responsible for the child after taking her to the Lycans and you kept watch over her as she grew. I understand that."

"From a distance, and I didn't spot her often. It wasn't until she was older that I had any direct contact with her again."

"Did you always feel drawn to her?"

Creed frowned, looking up again. "No. I was actually surprised she was attractive when she matured. She wasn't when I found her."

"That bad?"

"I couldn't even breathe through my nose. She hadn't been bathed and was pitiful as a child. I flew home immediately to shower and change my clothes after I gave her to the Lycan couple."

Lord Aveoth lifted a hand, waving Creed to his feet. He rose and locked his hands behind his back. His leader drew closer but remained distanced enough to keep out of striking range. Creed noticed. It implied he wasn't trusted.

"I spoke to Angel already. She said you threatened to fall to protect her."

"I will." He didn't have to think about it. "Please spare her."

"What of yourself? I'll give you the option to erase this mess by taking her life. You admitted it wasn't planned. Your bond is weak. Kill her, and you can resume your life as it was. I won't punish you."

Rage filled Creed. "No!"

Lord Aveoth narrowed his eyes. "Why not? You didn't want to mate her. She's human. That's going to displease your father. I'm giving you the option to fix this matter."

"I'll fall first." He tensed. "You can't punish her if I'm not here to see it. Please just send her back to her parents."

"You love her."

"I have feelings for her."

Lord Aveoth nodded. "You don't sound pleased about that."

"I would rather die than kill her. I'll do anything to protect her."

"Would you challenge me?"

Creed fisted his hands. "I would do anything to protect her," he repeated.

"Do you think you could win if we clashed swords?"

"No, my lord."

"But you'd still do it if I decided to have her killed?"

Hot rage flashed through him. "Yes. You would kill me, and there would be no reason for you to execute Angel."

"Stand down, Creed. I won't make you challenge me. Your Angel is safe from death."

He relaxed and unfurled his hands.

"She demanded she take your punishment. I agreed she could."

Creed dropped back to his knee and bowed. "I beg you not to do it! She wouldn't survive."

"Rise," Lord Aveoth thundered.

Creed stood. He jerked his head up and glared at his leader. "She'll die. She's too fragile to be lashed. She's also used to freedom. Her mind would snap in the dark after only a few weeks, if the blood loss doesn't kill her."

"I'm more than aware of human frailties." Lord Aveoth jerked his head toward the balcony. "Walk with me."

Creed kept his distance out of respect and followed his leader to the ledge. The sun was low in the sky, darkness near. Lord Aveoth sighed. "It's so beautiful here, isn't it?"

Creed nodded. He didn't give a damn about the weather or the view. "Please," he rasped. "I'll give you anything, do anything to spare Angel."

"Kelzeb told me that he shared what happened when I claimed my mate. Your father was one of the leading forces behind trying to get rid of me."

Creed suspected he'd see no mercy for Angel or for himself then. "I was informed."

"I hated Lord Abotorus. Killing him was a pleasure," Lord Aveoth softly admitted. "He was a cruel father to me, and a worse mate to my

179

mother. I wished for years that I was strong enough to challenge him, and then that day came. He planned to kill my mother. He wanted a son to replace me. I brought him shame. That's the kind of leader he was. He would have beheaded me as soon as his new vessel birthed a healthy boy."

He paused and crossed his arms over his chest. "I want the truth, Creed. It's just you and I here, as two men who were raised by the same types of men. Have you ever considered challenging your father?"

Creed looked at Aveoth. "Yes."

"Why haven't you?"

"My mother asked me not to. It would have hurt her. But she's no longer here. His cold indifference finally broke her heart and she died."

"Were you tempted to come back after her death and kill him?"

"Yes."

"And why didn't you?"

"My life wasn't my own to risk for personal reasons. It belongs to you. I am patient."

"He's the one who gifted the first hundred years of your life. You were given no choice."

"I still have honor."

Lord Aveoth nodded. "I now realize that. I admit to being leery at first. I don't know much about you since you're rarely here at the cliffs. I worried that you were like your father but you've proven you're not. You're a good man. That's why I changed the punishment for you mating your human. I am not Lord Abotorus, nor do I ever wish to be like him.

And you proved you're nothing similar to your father when you denied my offer to kill Angel. It was a test, Creed. You passed. Kado would have agreed without hesitation to kill his own mate to save his ass."

Creed faced his leader more. "What are you saying?"

"Your Angel is to take fifty hits to her backside with a paddle. It won't harm her too much and no permanent damage will be done. I also am giving her six months of confinement. I agree that no woman could or should be locked in darkness. She'll be assigned to living quarters instead of a cell."

Creed ducked his head, feeling shame. Angel would be hurt, and she was doing it for him. "I don't want her to suffer at all."

Aveoth gripped his arm. "I've made my decision. You've served me well. That's why I am choosing this exact punishment. It's not severe."

He nodded. "May I see her?"

"Yes. That is *your* punishment. You'll be there when she's paddled."

It would be one of the hardest things he'd ever had to do. "I understand."

"Will you attack the person who holds the paddle?"

"I will fight the urge. I know it would only make it worse for her and make the punishment begin anew."

"Follow me then. She's waiting. I've chosen one who is mated to do the deed."

Creed dreaded every step that took them to the lower guest quarters for visitors to the cliffs. He knew where she was kept when he saw a guard standing before a door. Aveoth motioned the guard off and it left them alone in the corridor.

"One more thing, Creed. Someone is covering your assignment but it's only temporary, until you leave here. I'm not letting you off your service to me for at least ten years. You know that territory and the people better than anyone, and I think your mate would appreciate being close to her parents. You may extend that time afterward if you wish, but we'll discuss that later."

Aveoth shifted his cloak and reached back, pulling something from his belt that had been hidden by his loose shirt. The paddle in his hand was smooth and fourteen inches long with a handle.

"I never said how hard she'd be hit. I'll leave that to you…but at least touch her skin." He held it out. "Fifty, Creed. Not one less. I'm going to trust you to do as I have decreed." He paused. "Once you are done here, there is clothing inside the wardrobe. Fly her down to your lair. Avoid the internal tunnels. I don't want any of the unmated to get a whiff of her. You'd have to fight your way home. The calling scent has been masked but it's still faintly there. She'll be confined to your lair, and you're to make certain she remains there until her sentence is served. You're her guard."

Creed was too stunned to move.

Aveoth smiled. "Do me one favor?"

"Anything." Creed accepted the paddle. It sank in that Aveoth was going to allow him to be the one to use it.

"Pretend to be miserable until you leave the cliffs. Grumble if anyone asks and tell them I felt being mated to a human would be punishment enough." He winked. "A lot of our people think Jill is pure hell for me. They have no idea how wrong they are. She's the best thing that's ever happened to me."

"Thank you." Emotion choked him. Lord Aveoth had done him the greatest kindness of all. "I swear."

Aveoth spun on his heel and walked away.

Creed closed his eyes and gripped the paddle with both of his hands. He had come home expecting the worst, possibly even death for him and Angel.

They were going to live, and not be parted. It was even a gift to be kept at his current assignment once the six months of confinement were over. Angel would get to remain with her pack, close to her parents.

Chapter Twelve

The door creaked open and Angel bit her lip. It was time to face the pain. She decided she wouldn't cry out no matter how much it hurt. GarLycans weren't the most emotional people. They probably suffered everything in silence. She would be brave for Creed. It might reflect badly on him if her screams were heard echoing down the tunnels.

The door slammed and she shifted her hands, wrapping her fingers around the chains attached to the leather restraints. It would give her something to concentrate on during the worst of it. Heavy-booted steps came closer and then stopped right behind her. She kept silent. It was probably best or she'd start babbling, maybe even crying.

She startled when wood barely bumped against her ass. She forced her body to relax as she took deep breaths. That was probably a practice swing to ensure so he wouldn't miss.

The second tap to her bottom was feather-light. Same for the third and fourth. Angel frowned. By the tenth, she understood that whoever held it was purposely not hurting her. He probably couldn't have stunned a fly with those taps. She relaxed more. He was mated. It was possible he couldn't bring himself to hurt a woman.

It was her lucky day. She refrained from saying words of gratitude. It might piss him off and make him hit her hard.

It ended on fifty, each tap as soft as the last. Wood hit the floor, and then she gasped when someone bent over her. The guy leaned against her back. There was no denying he had a hard-on when it pressed against her ass.

She struggled. "No!"

"Easy, Angel. I'm just releasing you."

It was Creed!

She threw her head forward, rubbing on the bed to get rid of the cloth over her face. Then she stared into his eyes, since he was right there next to her.

"Creed! That was you?"

"Yes." He smiled. "Lord Aveoth allowed me to be the one to spank you." He turned his head, using his outstretched arms to fumble with the buckles on each of her wrists. He got the right one free first.

"Why would he do that?"

He got her second arm free and straightened. He backed away and she stood, turning around. He'd changed his clothes, now sporting leather pants and a black long-sleeve shirt. She wanted to throw her arms around him, so she did, hugging him around his waist and burying her face against his chest. He held her back, hugging her tight.

"He had mercy."

"I only have to serve six months in jail."

"Inside my home with me."

She lifted her chin, stunned again.

"Lord Aveoth has been very generous. We need to go. I want to take you there now."

She hated to release him. The dress she'd discarded was on the floor and she bent to pick it up, but Creed gripped her arm, shaking his head.

"No." He let her go and strode to the wardrobe. He pulled out a red cape and opened it. "Come here."

He wrapped it around her like a blanket and scooped her into his arms. He hesitated and then shifted her, positioning her over his shoulder. "Stay still and be quiet."

"Okay." She didn't mind hanging from him. Creed had her.

He opened the door and quickly took them up a flight of stairs. They didn't pass anyone, that she could see, and then she knew they were close to an opening to the outside. It grew a bit colder and she could smell fresh air.

Creed bent and placed her on her feet, helping her keep the material together to protect her modesty. He stripped off his shirt next, tucking part of it into his pants. He scooped her up again to cradle in his arms. He closed his eyes while he allowed his wings to slide out. He opened them and rushed forward, jumping into the darkness.

Angel gasped. The sun had gone down outside and she couldn't see a thing. Creed halted their decent within seconds and continued flying downward in what seemed like a big circle. He landed somewhere but she still couldn't see a thing. He put her on her feet.

"Do not move. It's a small ledge and I have to open the door. You back up two feet and it's a fall. Step right and it's a fall."

"My feet are glued to this spot," she promised.

He no longer touched her and she heard what sounded like rock being shoved against rock. Creed returned to her fast and took her hand. He led her forward and she felt solid rock brush her side. The passage seemed tight for a short distance but then opened up. He stopped her.

"Stay."

"Okay."

"This is my home. I took us through the exterior door. I wasn't planning on returning so I didn't leave any lights on." His voice grew a little distant.

There was a click, and then blinding light came on from above.

Angel blinked, adjusting to being able to see again. It looked like a real home inside, with wood-paneled walls. She stood in the living room and there was a kitchen to her right. A long island separated the space.

Creed strode to her. "It will be more comfortable for you here than at the lair that overlooks your pack. I never spent much time updating it. I'll do that when we return." His wings were gone.

She didn't care where they were living. She did glance at how they'd gotten in. There was a big rock and it had been shoved away from the wall. Cool air came in. Creed followed her gaze and walked over to it, pressing a shoulder against the solid surface. He shoved, closing the space until the walls met.

"We seal them off when we aren't home. It makes it harder for anyone to find our lairs. It also keeps out the snow and cold in the winter."

"That looks heavy."

He shrugged. "It's only about six hundred pounds but it's on a track."

"Oh. Only."

He grinned. "Are you hungry?"

"A little."

"I don't have much here but I'll get you something." He held out his hand. "Come. I'll run you a bath."

"No thanks."

He arched his eyebrows.

"I already took one."

"Relax then. I'll go find you food. I'll be back."

She wanted to stop him but he moved too fast, walking across the room to a big door. "This is our home," he called out. "Be comfortable."

Then he was gone and she stood there, taking in the rooms. Creed had books on shelves on one wall. She walked toward them, staring at the ancient-looking volumes. She was afraid to touch them. She turned, following a hallway. The light switch was easy to locate and she flipped it on.

The first door opened into a small bedroom. It looked unused and smelled a little stale, as if the air hadn't been disturbed in a long time. She moved on, opening the door farther down. It was a bathroom. It wasn't large the way Gali's had been but it contained a shower and another claw-foot tub. The plumbing was almost modern, about thirty years out of date. She closed that door and opened the last one.

It was a bigger bedroom, and Creed's pants from earlier in the day were right inside the door on the floor. She found the light and entered.

He had a big bed, and there was a couch by a fireplace in the corner. She went to sit on it, just needing to take everything in. The cloak was big enough to use like a blanket as she adjusted it, wrapping it under her arms. Lord Aveoth had really been nice, if he was going to allow her to stay with Creed for her imprisonment. She smiled.

A door slammed, and she got up, hurrying out of the bedroom. "That was fast."

The man who stood in the living room brought her to a jarring halt.

It wasn't Creed. She knew who he was though, or at least who she guessed he had to be. They looked a lot alike.

She cleared her throat, not sure what to say to Creed's father. He said nothing, but he didn't have to. His lips pressed firmly together and he made a loud grumbling noise of disapproval. She backed up.

"Where is my son?"

She winced as his voice rose to a yell. "He went to get me something to eat."

His nostrils flared. "You dare speak to me?"

"You asked a question. I answered."

"Insolence!"

She backed up a little more.

He pointed at her. "You have ruined my plans for my son. He threw everything away for *you*!"

Well, she wasn't going to get along with her new father-in-law. It didn't exactly break her up. He seemed like an asshole.

"In forty years, he would have taken his place as one of the palace enforcers. Now he'll be demoted and shamed. For what?" He glared at her body. "A puny human breeder. It's an insult to our line!"

189

She took another step back, moving slow when he began to pace, breaking eye contact with her.

"I will not allow it to happen. I can salvage this... He went to get her food! He's become an errand runner for a *human*." He threw back his head and bellowed.

She was tempted to run but there was nowhere to go. He could break through the doors. He was a full-blooded Gargoyle. She just held still, hoping he'd forget she was even there, or that Creed would return.

The man resumed pacing, his hands locked together behind his back. He shot her a furious look. "My mating with a Lycan was a mistake. His mate will be a pure-blood like myself. It will wean out the weakness in *his* children that became known in my own. My second mate will be one as well, so my future sons shall be born strong."

Oh shit. That didn't sound good. She glanced at the door Creed had left through, starting to pray he'd come back before his old man decided to kill her. It looked as if it was heading that way.

"I knew it was a mistake to make an alliance with those Lycans." He spun her way. "Even humans were better than them. Do you know why?"

She shook her head, afraid he'd go off if she spoke or didn't respond at all.

"Their bloodlines are weaker and our traits come through cleaner." He scanned her from head to foot again. "Perhaps my son isn't dense after all. I never told him I planned to find him a pure-blood mate. He may have seen the same problem with Lycans that I did." He stormed toward her, and she pressed tight against the wall.

He passed her, stomping down the hallway. She debated on following him but didn't. She watched him enter Creed's bedroom. He wasn't in there long. He came toward her again and she bolted to the only place she could go. She put the kitchen island between them and turned, hoping he wasn't going to lunge across it to do something bad. It also gave her time to tighten the cape around her body.

He paced in the living room. Angel glanced around, looking for a weapon, but then discarded the idea. He could shell out his skin and it would just break the knife if she stabbed him. He'd kill her for sure. She held still, watching him.

The door opened and Creed entered, carrying a bag. One glimpse at them both and he dropped it, hurrying forward.

"Father. What are you doing here?"

"I came to see if it was true. You mated a human."

Creed put his body between her and his father from the other side of the island. "I did."

"You have not chained her. You don't even have them readily available. I looked."

"She's my mate."

"They are unstable creatures. You must chain her when you leave. She could attempt to escape."

"Angel isn't going to do that. I didn't force the mating. She is with me of her own free will."

His father snorted. "It's what they do. Their feeble minds can't withstand what we are. She'll go insane and try to hurt herself or your child when you get her pregnant."

"I didn't invite you here and I want you to leave. You aren't to enter my lair without prior permission—and *never* when I am not here."

"You dare speak to me that way?"

Creed advanced until they were almost chest to chest. They were the same size in bulk and height. "I dare."

"Back down!" his father thundered.

Angel grabbed for her ears, covering them. She glanced around, expecting to see cracks in the walls or something. Nothing happened. She watched the pair of men glaring at each other, now that she felt secure the roof wouldn't come down on top of them. Creed's lair at the cliffs seemed stronger than the one that rested above her village.

"Get out," Creed demanded. "I will not take orders from you."

"You are my son. You *will* obey me!"

"I won't." Creed softened his tone to almost a whisper. "Mother isn't here to stop me anymore from fighting you. You allowed her to wither and die. How could you?"

The elder man turned a little gray-skinned. So did Creed. Angel wondered if the living room was about to become a battleground. She worried about Creed but they looked evenly matched. Creed was younger though, possibly giving him the advantage. Neither of them spoke for a long time.

"I didn't wish for that to happen," the elder finally admitted. "I think of her often. Her death wasn't foreseen."

"Don't pretend you care. I'm not fooled by your act. I will always put my mate first. I won't allow you to come in here. Do you understand? You are misery that walks. I won't have you tainting my Angel."

"Chain her then. Keep the rock in place so she doesn't plunge to her death the first time you decide to breed her for a youngling, after revealing what you are to her."

"She's seen me. Angel knows exactly what I am. Now get out."

The father turned his head, studying Angel. "You don't believe he's a demon?"

"Am I allowed to speak now?" She wasn't about to forget the last time she'd answered him.

"I give my permission."

Creed growled.

"Thanks." Angel didn't want them to fight. "Yes, I know what Creed is, and I'm never going to leap to my death. Count on that. If I ever go off a ledge, it's because I was pushed or thrown."

"He can change forms and fly. Were you aware of that, human? I am betting he made sure you couldn't see him when he mated you."

"Actually, you are wrong. I think he's sexy when he's gray and has wings." She even reached up to shove the cape away and reveal skin, tapping the healing wound from where he'd bitten her to make a point. "We mated facing each other. The fangs are hot too."

193

His father grimaced and glared at Creed. "She's already not of sound mind."

"She is."

"I was raised in a Lycan pack," she added. "Biting is normal. So is partially shifting when in heat. It happens sometimes. I'm not afraid of Creed. I love him."

"Love?" the elder spat and his eyes turned black. "That's why you mated her? She has feelings for you? It mattered?"

"It always matters," Creed grumbled. "Get out. I won't say it again. You do not have permission to come into my lair or be anywhere near my mate. I'll fight you if you do."

"You're flawed." Creed's father backed away from him, stepped to the side and stormed out. He slammed the door when he left.

Creed lowered his head and Angel moved around the island. "It's okay." She stopped in front of him, staring into his eyes. He looked miserable. She put her hands on his chest. "I'm sorry."

"Did he frighten you? Threaten you? Touch you? I'll kill him if he laid a finger on you."

"I'm good. He kept his distance and just yelled a lot." She wasn't about to repeat anything his father had said. It might hurt him more.

"I'm sorry you had to witness that."

"You saw where I came from before you took me to the village. I was the poster child for fucked-up parenting and bad beginnings. He's no reflection on you. It doesn't matter what he thinks."

"I'm a disappointment to him."

194

"Who cares? He's an asshole." She softened her tone. "I love you." She slid her hands up his chest and gripped his shoulders. "Take me to bed. I can make you forget all about him."

The silver in his eyes flared to life, shining. "Is that your solution? I nearly challenged my father to fight to the death and you wish to lure me to bed?"

"Yes. Do you have a problem with that?"

His lips twitched, almost a smile. "No."

"Good. I'm in the mood to celebrate, and that means getting you naked. I can't think of a better way."

"Celebrate?"

"My ass isn't burning from pain and I'm not locked up in some black hole. The only marks that're going to be on your back will be from my nails if you're really good in bed." She smiled. "Don't disappoint me. That's all you have to worry about. Otherwise, I'll have meant it when I said I'd have to train you."

His lips curved upward and it melted her when he grinned like that. "You said fucking me would be torture."

"Absolutely. Torture me, baby. I look forward to it."

"Let me lock the door. I don't want him to come back."

"Good idea." She let him go and backed away.

"I brought food."

"I want you more. We'll eat later."

"I have to put this away or it will go bad. Some of it is fresh meat."

"Hurry. I'll meet you in the bedroom."

"I will."

He strode to the door and bolted it. She watched him bend to pick up the bag he'd brought before she rushed down the hallway. The bed beckoned and she climbed on, fumbling to get rid of the cape. She tossed the material on the floor and then glanced at the four posts. They were almost thick enough to be considered pillars. She stood on the bed, walking to one at the foot.

Creed entered and started stripping, his gaze fixed on her. "The calling is fainter."

"It's this stuff they dipped me in when I arrived. That's why I probably made a face when you mentioned taking a bath. I can relate to fried foods now."

He bent down, tearing off his boots. "I don't understand."

"My mother dips meat in milk and egg, then breads it. I felt like that, minus the sticky part."

He straightened and approached. It was nice to be taller than him for once. He wrapped one of his hands around her waist and leaned in, burying his face against her chest. He inhaled. "I see."

"Do I stink? My nose doesn't pick it up but yours is more sensitive."

"No. It faintly masks your scent. I pick up natural oils, a little maple, and—"

"Don't tell me the rest. I don't want to know if it's something gross."

He turned his head, rubbing his cheek against the side of her breast. "There won't be hormones this time. I'll be gentler with you."

She slid her fingers into his hair and he lifted his chin. "Don't hold back with me. Ever. Just be you, Creed."

"Are you certain?"

"Yes."

He seemed to study her eyes and then released her, backing away. "Tell me if it gets too intense."

She grinned. "Do you want to use a safe word?"

"What is that?" He started unfastening his pants.

"Humans pick a word to call out if the sex gets too rough."

He scowled. "I don't want to know any more."

"What's wrong?"

"It reminds me that you've had lovers."

"I'm sure you have too."

He rumbled deep in his chest. "Only during the ravage. One, who wasn't you. Don't ever tell me anything about the lovers you've had, Angel. I'll track them down and kill them. I wouldn't want you to hate me for doing that."

He was jealous. "Creed?"

He held her stare.

"You're the only man I've ever loved. Nothing else matters."

"You'd let me kill them?"

She inwardly winced. That wouldn't be good. No one should die just because she'd slept with them. "They don't matter enough to kill," she stated honestly.

197

He bent, shoving down his pants. She released the bedpost and backed up to sit on the bed. Creed rid himself of his pants and lunged forward. He grabbed her ankle before she could react. He gripped the other one and pulled. Angel gasped, falling flat on the mattress.

"You're mine now. No one else will ever touch you again." He jerked her down the bed toward him.

She wasn't afraid. Creed bent her legs when he ran his hands up them to her thighs. He parted them, using his hold to drag her a little closer. She lifted her head, noticing he was aroused. There was no missing Creed with a hard-on.

"I'm not skilled but I'm motivated," he rasped. "I researched human sex."

That surprised her. "You did?"

His eyes were swirling silver. "I couldn't have you but I thought about it often." He glanced down at her pussy. "I daydreamed about what it would be like if I ever had you in my bed. I wanted it to be good for you. I bought books women wrote on pleasing them. I knew they'd have the best advice."

She'd thought he'd never wanted her but that confession proved her wrong. It must have been a lot of trouble for him to do that. It wasn't like they had bookstores in the village. He probably had to order them by internet or travel to a bigger city to find them. The fact that he would go to that much trouble for her meant everything. He did love her.

He held her stare. "Am I making you sad?"

"No. The opposite. That's so sweet, Creed. You did that for me?"

"You don't go into heat the way a Lycan does. I never dreamed you would volunteer for the ravage. It meant if I ever took you to bed that I'd have to know how to make you wet and ready to take me."

"Keep talking and I'm there."

"I haven't even told you how beautiful I think you are. The book stated I should tell you how you affect me." He glanced down at his stiff cock. "Besides the physical indications."

"Just kiss me and let me touch you. That will do it."

"I will never forget the feel of your mouth on me. I want to do the same to you. It brought me such pleasure."

"Okay. I'm not going to talk you out of that." She bit her lip. "Did you research sexual positions? I've never done sixty-nine but we could give it a shot."

"I did. It would be too distracting. Tell me if I do this wrong."

He bent forward, spreading her thighs more. Angel held her breath as she watched him get closer to her pussy. He released her thighs and shoved his hands under her ass, lifting it a little. Then his mouth was on her.

He had a hot, wet tongue. He was hesitant at first, tracing it upward from her slit to her clit. She reached down, lightly touching his hair by stroking it. She kept her legs wide apart to give him plenty of room. He found the spot and she moaned.

"There."

He stopped and lifted his head. "Yes?"

"Oh yeah. Zone in right there and you have me."

He actually smiled. "Up and down or circles?"

"Either way."

"I'll figure it out." He dipped his head, his mouth returning to her clit. He applied more pressure but was teasing with the tip of his tongue, almost playing.

Angel closed her eyes. "A little rougher," she urged.

He complied and she moaned, releasing his hair so she didn't pull it. She gripped her thighs instead to keep from slamming them shut on his face when it started to feel too good.

"Can you growl for me? Lycan style?"

He growled and it added vibrations. She moaned louder and knew she wasn't going to last long. Creed was a fast learner. Her nipples tightened and she reached up, running a hand over one. He pulled her closer or buried his face more, she wasn't sure which. It made it feel even better. Ecstasy struck and she cried out his name as she came.

Creed stopped growling and lifted his face, easing her ass to the bed. "Your taste makes me so hard."

She opened her eyes, staring into his silver ones. "A-plus," she panted.

He arched one eyebrow and removed his hands from under her ass. He traced his finger over the seam of her pussy. "You're wet now. What is A-plus?"

"The best grade you could get. You pass oral sex training," she joked.

He moved his hand and gripped her thighs, dragging her ass to the end of the bed. He entered her in one slow thrust. She loved watching his

200

face, almost as much as the feel of how big and wonderful his cock felt inside her. He closed his eyes, his fangs extending. His lips were parted so she could see them. He held her legs as he started to move in and out of her.

"This should be outlawed," he groaned.

She reached up and cupped her breasts, massaging them. "Watch."

He opened his eyes and noticed what she did. He started to fuck her faster, pounding in and out of her. He adjusted his hold and gripped the tops of her bent thighs to hold her in place.

She arched her back, licking her lips. "You're so hard. You feel so good."

His skin started to pale and shade gray. He froze, breathing heavy. "It feels too good. It's excessively stimulating."

Frustration rose. "Don't do that." She moved her legs, hooking them around his hips to pull him close and making his cock go inside her deeper. "Let go, Creed. Be yourself. Feel for me. Don't hold back."

He bowed his head. "It's wrong to feel this much."

She shook her own. "There's no one here but us. No one is going to see, Creed. Let go, baby. It's called passion, and we're mates." She rocked her hips, moving him inside her. It made her moan. "Fuck me. Give me everything you've got."

His eyes were so amazing when they were swirling silver, almost glowing, as if they had a life of their own. He looked down at her breasts. She rubbed them again, showing him how her nipples responded.

"Angel." It sounded like a warning.

"Are you about to lose control?"

"Yes."

"Good. Lose it."

It was all the urging he needed. He shoved her hands out of the way. His chest pinned hers and he started to fuck her. She wrapped her legs higher around his waist. She found his back, raking her nails over it. The slits that were usually smooth over his shoulder blades ridged out and she knew he was about to sprout wings. She moved her hands lower, down to his spine, to give them room if they did. His cock felt harder and thicker. She lifted her head, kissing his shoulder. It was hard to focus on him when she wanted to come. She fought it though. It was more about him at that moment.

He buried his face against her throat, moans tearing from his parted lips. His fangs touched her and she moved her head in the opposite direction. "Yes," she urged, panting.

He bit. The slight pain, added to the mounting pleasure, sent her over the edge. She cried out his name, holding on tight as she climaxed. Creed's jaw clamped down and he fucked her harder, faster. Then he threw his head back, letting her go with his fangs. He groaned as he found his own release.

Angel smiled, trying to think around her body tingling from being loved by her mate. His wings had come out and they were resting over the top of her legs wrapped around his waist. She glanced at his skin. He was grayish in color but his flesh had remained supple and warm.

"A-plus and bonus credit for the velvet rubbing against my skin." She knew he'd understand what she meant. His wings were that soft.

He chuckled.

Chapter Thirteen

The fire coming from the fireplace across the room gave off a romantic atmosphere. Angel finished her last piece of elk. Creed had brought in more pillows from the spare bedroom and both of them sat up in bed, cushioned from the headboard.

"Thank you. I didn't even know you could cook." She flashed him a smile. "It was really good."

"I've lived alone since I was a small youngling. I don't like to eat it fresh from the bone. The scouts taught me how to cook."

"You didn't get the craving for raw meat from your mother?"

"No. I enjoy my meals cooked."

"Me too. I always had to glance away when someone from the pack captured and immediately ate a rabbit or something. Raw meat is gross." She moved her legs, untangling them from his bedding. "Thank you. It was so thoughtful of you to start a fire and then fix me dinner."

"You're my mate." He used a napkin to dab at her chin.

"You're spoiling me."

"You deserve that and so much more."

She studied his eyes. "How are you doing?"

"Why do you ask?"

"We just spent two hours messing up your bed and this is our first night as mates. I know how *I* feel, but I'm wondering about you."

"I like this."

"Good."

He took her plate and twisted away, placing it on a table he'd carried in. He faced her again. "I would like to discuss something with you."

"Okay. Hit me."

He scowled. "Never."

"It's a saying."

"I don't like that one."

She grinned. "What do you want to talk about?"

"There're two subjects we need to cover as new mates."

She was curious. "What are they?"

"I just thought of another. Three subjects."

"Okay."

He pulled away from the pillows to get a better look at her face. "Will you take my blood? It will strengthen the bond."

"Yes."

"You don't have fangs. I'll have to bleed for you."

She nodded. "I'm sorry about that. I'm familiar with it since my parents told me what mates do. You'll need to cut yourself so I can get the blood."

"Never apologize. It's a custom of ours to share blood that way. We don't bite into someone unless it's to take their blood to trigger the mating process. I bit you tonight because we're still bonding. Once it's complete, I won't have that urge anymore."

"I didn't know that."

"I'd like for you to sleep in my bed with me."

That surprised her. "Was there ever a doubt?"

"We keep our own bedchambers. That's our custom."

"That one sucks, so no, I'm not sleeping apart from you. I'd have fought with you'd tried to put me in another room. I'd have just climbed into bed with you after you had fallen asleep. Try to keep me away from you."

He smiled. "Good. I like having you close, and I'd worry about you being cold or frightened in another room."

"That has nothing to do with my reasons. I just want to hold you."

His expression softened. "I want that as well."

"You said three. What's the third?"

He reached out and placed his hand on her stomach. "Children. We need to decide if you should eat the root or not."

"The what?"

"It's our form of birth control for humans. I asked a scout I trust about how to avoid pregnancy happening while I went to get food. He said he could get it for me if I wanted. You need to start eating it, since I've mated you. You need to take a bite of the root every day. Our sperm is very strong when we go into the ravage or when we first take a mate. You're putting off the calling scent and my body responds to that by trying very hard to impregnate you."

"So you're saying you have super-sperm right now?"

He nodded.

"This root works as a contraceptive?"

"Yes."

Angel placed her hand on her stomach, imagining what it would be like to have Creed's baby. The thought wasn't a bad one. She liked the idea. "Do you want kids?"

His eyes were blue at that moment but they sparked with silver, as if lightening were striking inside the irises. "I would be honored if you did. You're human, so there's a higher chance you can get pregnant since you can't control your ovulation cycles."

"I don't think so. I'm on the shot. It's a human form of birth control. I haven't taken your blood yet except for when I bit you. I don't think that was enough though. Once I do, it can mess with it. Otherwise, in a month it won't be good anymore. That's when I'm due to have another shot."

His lips compressed into a tight line.

"What?"

"Why were you on it? No—don't answer that. I don't want to know." He looked away.

"I have the worst periods ever," she admitted. "Cramps. I get PMS. It's bad. I'll cry, then burst into a bitch fit of major proportions over stupid shit. It's not pretty. That's why I started taking the shot and stay on it. It prevents me from having periods."

He held her gaze. "It wasn't because you had a lover before you came home to the pack? Is he waiting for you to return?"

"No."

He rubbed her stomach. "I would like to leave it to nature."

She understood his meaning. "That's fine with me."

"You wouldn't feel ill at ease if you got pregnant?"

She didn't laugh at the way he put it. She translated it into freaking out. "To have a little version of you? No." She clasped his hand over her belly. "Never. As you said, it would be an honor."

"It's a new concept to me, contemplating having a youngling. I believed I wouldn't have to consider it until after my hundredth birthday."

"You'll make a wonderful father."

He looked away. "I have my doubts."

"Hey?" She reached up and grabbed his jaw, turning his face back. She held his gaze. "You *will* make an amazing father. Trust me on that."

"I never wish to be like my own."

"You won't be."

He grew silent.

"I'm going to tell you what my mother said to me. I had this freak-out moment once about what kind of mother I'd be one day if I ever had kids. My biological one took off, remember? She abandoned me to that place where you found me. Just left me to that hell. I was worried I might have inherited bad traits. See where I'm going with this? Do you want to know the advice my mother shared?"

He leaned into her hand, watching her. "Yes."

"Life is what you make it. You take the bad you've experienced or seen and learn what not to do later in life. Who you become is up to you. The past is just that. You let it go and move forward. You are going to be a fantastic father."

"I lack in the ability to show emotion."

"That's why you have me. We'll have time to work on it, Creed." She smiled. "You've come a long way. Could you imagine us in bed together like this a month ago, doing the things we just did?"

He smiled back. "No."

"See? And this is our second night together. You build walls and I'll break them down. I won't let you close yourself off ever again."

"You will tell me if I'm too cold? I worry I might not meet your needs."

She leaned in closer. "You meet and exceed them." She brushed her lips over his. "Trust me."

He stroked her cheek. "You are everything to me."

"I love you too."

She closed her eyes, deepening the kiss. He kissed her back. He was a fast learner in this regard, as well. He pulled her closer, his big hands roaming her body. He used his elbow to shove the pillows out of the way, dragging her down with him to lie flat. She pushed the sheets away to reach more of his skin, doing some touching of her own.

Creed broke the kiss. "Blood."

It took her a second to cool her desire enough to let what he'd said sink in and make sense. "Now? Later."

"Now."

"You have the worst timing." She slapped his chest. "I wanted to ride you."

"I didn't say you couldn't." Amusement sparked in his eyes. "I want to feed you first."

"You already did. You fed me elk steak and whatever that white stuff was. I couldn't decide if it was mashed rice or potato. It was good though. The green stuff in it kind of confused my taste buds."

He rolled, pinning her under him. "You need to take my blood on a full stomach. Otherwise your digestive system won't accept it as easily. This is the time."

She stuck out her lower lip and pouted. "You're so mean. All I want to do is ride you like a pony."

He smiled. "I'm a stallion, baby." He lifted off her, getting off the bed.

Angel laughed. Her normally stony GarLycan was playing with her. "Come back to bed. I can drink it later."

He crossed the room and left the bedroom. She sat up after he was gone, liking it when he walked away from her. He did have the nicest ass.

He was determined to strengthen their bond. His timing did suck but he was the sensible one. Her digestive system would reject blood on an empty stomach. She'd throw it back up.

He returned with a tray. Angel frowned.

He sat on the edge of the bed and set it down. There was a silver, thin, fluted champagne glass and a dagger. Her eyebrows arched. "What's this?"

He picked up the dagger. "I cut and bleed into the goblet. You drink from it."

She grabbed his wrist, halting the sharp weapon. "Are you serious?"

"It's customary."

"Your people are so formal."

He just stared at her.

"Give me the dagger." She held out her other hand. "Let's do this in a more fun way."

"I'm worried to see what that is."

"You heal fast and you know I'd never hurt you. Trust me."

He hesitated, and then handed over the dagger to her handle first. "I do."

"Get rid of the glass and tray."

He stood, taking them around the bed to the table. She pointed at the bed and he climbed on. She was careful with the sharp-tipped dagger as she crawled closer to him.

"Flat on your back."

He did it but frowned. "What is your plan?"

She set the dagger down and bent over him, brushing kisses on his stomach. He hissed out when she trailed them lower, going toward his groin.

"Don't slice me there."

She laughed. "No. Never, ever there. Only my mouth is going to touch the good parts."

He reached up, caressing her breast. "I appreciate that."

She licked the hollow of his hip, staring at his cock. He was getting hard. She moved closer and nibbled on his lower stomach. "It's about to get a lot better."

She lifted her leg, throwing it over one of his. He spread his thighs to give her more room. She gripped the shaft of his cock and opened her mouth, flicking her tongue over the tip. She looked up at him, meeting his gaze. His eyes were swirling silver but some blue still showed. It was almost neon. He had the sexiest eyes and responses to oral sex. He pinched her nipple and it caused her to jerk. It didn't hurt, but she knew he'd done it to get her attention. She liked it.

She took him inside her mouth, sucking lightly. His fangs extended and she hoped he didn't sprout wings flat on his back. She wasn't even sure if he could or if it would hurt. She took him deeper, watching his eyes narrow. Soft noises came from the back of his throat. His chest rumbled. She slowly released him and lifted her chest, climbing up his body. She positioned his shaft at the angle she wanted when she straddled his hips and sat, taking him deep inside her pussy. He grabbed her hips.

"Angel," he moaned.

"Definitely not a pony." She rose up a little, slamming back down.

He tightened his hold, pleasure showing on his features. "Blood later."

She leaned over, grabbing the dagger. "No. Now. Give me your hand."

He shook off some of the lust and sat up a little. He only hesitated for a second before giving her his hand. She gripped it.

"Remember what I was just doing to you with my mouth?"

"Yes."

"Close your eyes and just feel. Think about my mouth on you."

She hated to cut him. She moved her hips, slowly riding his cock. It felt amazing to her, and she hoped the pleasure distracted him. He fell back flat on the bed. His other hand gripped her hip, kneading her skin there.

She used the tip of the dagger to slice his thumb deep. He didn't even flinch. Red blood welled up.

She tossed the dagger off the bed and lifted his hand, wrapping her mouth around his digit, sucking. The taste of his blood filled her mouth and she swallowed. She did to his thumb what she'd done to his cock earlier as she slowly moved, riding him.

He grew harder inside her, felt bigger. She moaned against his thumb, feeling secure that it was working the way she'd wanted it to. Taking blood was going to be fun for both of them.

Her body started to heat up and sweat broke over her. It was probably from taking his blood. It happened with Lycans, and she remembered his mother had been one. She moved faster, frantically. She was close to coming. Her clit throbbed and she reached down with her other hand, rubbing her fingertip against it. She sucked on his thumb harder.

Creed snarled and bucked under her, ramming his cock inside her. He almost unseated her but his hand gripping her hip helped avoid that. She cried out, climaxing hard.

She rode him and he sat up suddenly, wrapping his arm around her waist. He tore his thumb from her mouth, holding her with that arm too. She was crushed against him. He threw them to the side on the bed, his hips pumping furiously as he came. He clung to her as he shook from the force of his climax.

Chapter Fourteen

Creed adjusted a little so he wasn't squeezing Angel so tightly. It took him time to recover. "Did I hurt you?"

"Let's do that again."

He couldn't resist laughing. She made him feel so many emotions. It was getting easier to stop stifling them with her in his arms. She was life and light. Pleasure and...pain. It stabbed at his chest at the mere thought of losing her.

He would never allow that to happen. She was his mate.

He brushed her hair back and lifted his head, looking at her face. She was pure splendor, all contained within one small body with fragile bones. Her blue eyes stared back at him and he saw the teasing light in them. "I liked your plan much better than mine."

"And here I was worried I would have to chain you down and seduce you just to get sex if you weren't in the ravage thing. I'm so glad I was wrong."

She humbled him. She wanted him despite not knowing much about of his kind. Not once had she shown a sliver of regret that he'd mated her. He hadn't even asked her permission. "You are remarkable."

"So are you."

"I need you to make me a promise, one you will always keep. Your honor." He worried about her.

"Anything."

He tried to find the right words. It was difficult. "Tell me if I sadden you or begin to crush your spirit. I'll do anything to avoid that."

She sobered. "I will, but that's never going to happen."

He wasn't so sure. He would try to be more open with her and show her how much she meant to him. He silently made that pledge.

She wrapped her arms more firmly around him. "I'm nothing like your mother."

It shouldn't have surprised him that she'd guess where his thoughts lay. Angel seemed to know him too well.

"You're nothing like your father, either." She stroked his hair. "I met him, remember?"

He closed his eyes and nuzzled his face into the crook of her neck. "I hope I'm not."

"Creed, listen to me." She kept running her fingers through his hair, rubbing his skin near his shoulder with her other hand. "You make me happy. I wouldn't let you shut me out. I'd get in your face to yell, or drop to my knees if you ever grew cold. Try to ignore me while you're getting a blow job. Good luck with that."

He barked out a laugh. He could imagine her doing something that outlandish. His Angel wasn't timid.

"See? You're laughing. Your dick is currently hardening inside me just thinking about it. Oh yeah. We're naked in bed together, still connected intimately, hugging each other. I can guarantee your father was never in this position with your mother. Not to gross you out by mentioning your parents had to have sex for you to be here, but you know what I mean. You're nothing like him."

She had a point. "He chained her every time. He never allowed her to touch him when they bred."

"I'm not surprised. You aren't him, Creed. You always say you're more Gargoyle than Lycan, but I think *he* told you that because it's what he wanted to see. You do have a heart. You also have passion and kindness. Those are things he'll never be accused of possessing. You take after your mother."

He hoped that was true.

"You held it all in because it was expected of you. Well, I'm telling you to let it all out. You can. It's safe here with me."

He wished it were that simple. "It's weakness."

"No. It's strength. There's nothing more frightening than laying your emotions bare to someone else. You risk being hurt. I'm never going to cause you heartache. I love you."

He held her tighter. "I've hurt you before."

She was quiet for long seconds. "I can't say you haven't. You broke my heart when you stopped talking to me. I never stopped loving you though. That's the only way you could hurt me. Don't shut me out again."

"Never," he swore.

"Then we're good."

"I won't always know the right words to say or I may react to things in a way that disappoints you."

216

"That's okay. I'm not shy about telling you how I feel and I can be demanding. I'll let you know if you drop the ball."

"What if I do something you can't forgive?"

She seemed to take her time thinking that over. "Don't cheat on me. I know you'd never hit me. Those are the only two things that are deal breakers. I might be pissed if you forget my birthday but that just means you'll have to buy me a better gift."

"You know I'd never be unfaithful or strike you."

"I do know. That's the point."

He lifted his head, holding her gaze. "I can't ever lose you. I don't believe I could survive."

"I love you too, Creed. You won't."

"If I had a heart, you would be it."

She slid one of her hands down to his chest. "Then I'm right here. You do have a heart. You'll say the words one day. I can wait."

"It hurts you." He disappointed her already.

"No." She smiled. "You might stumble over the L word but you show me how you feel with the things you say and in the way you touch me. I hear it and feel it."

"I would do anything for you."

"See? That's love."

"I'm already failing you as a mate."

"Shut up." She lifted her hand and pressed it over his mouth. "Just listen. I love you exactly how you are. I don't expect you to be some flowery poet type or to be perfect. I don't want that. I want *you*. You're

217

grumpy and moody a lot. Hell, you piss me off. Like now. That's okay. I still love you. You aren't going to convince me it was a mistake to mate you. I'm not sorry in the least. I'm happy. Well, right now I'm irritated but you know what I mean. Stop obsessing about what you think you're going to do in the future. You are nothing like that walking misery, as you called him. I'm not like your mother, either. She allowed him to hurt her until she lost the will to live. That's what you said. Can you ever see me suffering in silence? I never shut up." She released his mouth. "Got it?"

He grinned. "Yes."

She smiled back. "Get the rocks out of your head, GarLycan. You're stuck with me for centuries."

"Gargoyles can live for millennia. I do physically take after them."

Her eyes widened. "Even their mates?"

"You'll live as long as I do. My blood will assure that."

"Wow. That shocks me but I admit I don't hate the idea of being able to live thousands of years with you. Then we have plenty of time to make sure our relationship works."

He nodded. "We will."

"Don't worry so much. I appreciate it and it shows you're concerned about me. See? Those aren't actions of a man who is cold. You care too much, and that proves you're nothing like your father."

"Thank you for saying that."

She yawned. "Do you know what I need?"

"Sleep?"

She nodded. "In your bed. With you. I want you to hold me. Is that going to be too weird? I know you're used to being alone. If so, I'll wait until you're sleeping and just curl into you."

"I think I can handle it." He maneuvered out of her arms and separated their bodies. "I'm going to take the dishes into the kitchen. I'll be right back."

"Hurry." She stretched, and he loved seeing her body that way. She didn't try to hide it from him.

He picked up the dagger so she didn't step on it if she got up during the night and collected their plates. He hurried into the kitchen, rinsing them. He'd do dishes later. He wanted to get back to her.

A light tap on the door distracted him, and he frowned. He walked over to the door though and unbolted it, keeping most of his body hidden when he peered out. He'd kill his father if it was him.

Kelzeb stood there. "You're up. I didn't want to pound in case you had already retired."

"I had. I was out of bed for a moment."

"May I come in?"

Creed sighed. "I'm nude."

Kelzeb chuckled. "If you have something I haven't seen before, I'm curious enough to want a peek." He glanced both ways, his humor vanishing. "It's important. I would have tried to reach you again at dawn but didn't want to let this sit for that long."

"Give me ten seconds before you enter."

Creed spun, walked into the living room and glanced around. He bent, picking up one of the carpet runners and just wrapping it around his waist. He put his body between the front door and the hallway to the bedroom, hoping that Angel wouldn't seek him out.

The front door opened wider and Kelzeb stepped inside, closing it behind him.

"I apologize. You're strengthening your bond but this couldn't wait."

"What is wrong? Is it my father?"

"How did you know?"

"We had a confrontation. He came to see me here. What has he done?"

"Kado made a formal written request to go before Aveoth. He's outraged that you broke the law and aren't being lashed and encased. He petitioned for your mate to be enslaved and requested that, since he's your father, he get to be the first to use her body as a breeding vessel. The prick feels it's his right to have first crack at it since he's lost a son over her."

Creed started to shell. Rage poured through him. His skin hardened and he couldn't breathe. He knew his father wasn't pleased but the petition was one he'd never seen coming.

"Easy," Kelzeb ordered. "It won't happen. Aveoth is almost as angry as you must be. Hell, so am I. It's your right as her mate to be informed of what's going on, so you can be there to represent her and yourself."

That helped. He got air into his lungs and some of the rage died down. He relaxed his body, trying to regain control.

"I don't know what his next move will be, but first thing in the morning he's going to go before Aveoth, and he'll be denied on all counts. Seven o'clock sharp if you plan to attend. I never saw this coming, and it's my job to think of ways we might have any problems with our clan. I can't even wrap my head around him coming up with this scheme. It's like one of those messed-up talk shows on television or a soap opera. Perhaps he's watched too many of them in his down time. He's trying to make you your half-brother's stepfather."

Creed scowled.

"You don't watch those? I probably shouldn't either." He glanced around. "I don't even see a television. You're barely here, so you probably didn't take the time to get one." He held Creed's gaze. "Your mate's rights would be stripped from that baby if she were a breeding vessel, so you wouldn't technically be the child's stepfather, but if your father was the youngling's father then it *would* make you the half-brother. See where I'm going with this?"

"No."

"Never mind. Just watch that bastard father of yours and don't leave your mate unprotected."

"Thank you. I won't."

Kelzeb sighed. "I'll text you a copy of that video of Aveoth stripping him of his rank. It might keep you from hunting him down tomorrow after the audience with Aveoth."

"Doubtful."

"Contact me if you do decide to defend his formal request. Aveoth is going to deny it, so you don't have to be there."

221

"I don't need to think about it. I want to face him when he speaks to Lord Aveoth."

"I'll send someone to guard your mate at that time. She's not supposed to leave your lair. She won't be allowed to join you. You also don't want to fight your father anywhere near her. I've learned that two of your brothers are with him now. I've had a few enforcers watching them since the formal request came in. They are probably plotting their next move."

"Do you know which two?"

"The two above you nearest in age. The eldest one didn't fly home."

That didn't surprise Creed. Those two probably had hope that they may one day achieve their father's approval. Though his brothers may just be humoring their father by listening to his rantings in their attempt. His oldest brother wouldn't bother. Nebulas hated him almost as much as Creed did. "I will challenge him over this."

"I don't blame you." Kelzeb turned, walking to the door. "Lock down your lair. I wouldn't put it past them to attack in the middle of the night. Kado is a sneaky bastard, and if he's smart, he knows he'll be denied by Aveoth."

Creed followed him to the door and bolted it when he exited. He turned, staring at the wall across the room that hid the exterior ledge. His father and brothers knew the location of the outside entrance. He dropped the rug he'd used to cover himself and walked to the couch, lifting it. He wedged it in place. They wouldn't be able to slide the rock to sneak in without snapping the couch frame.

He strode into the kitchen, getting some glasses to place on one arm of the couch. They would fall to the floor and shatter if the couch was nudged, as an extra precaution.

He crept down the hallway and found Angel curled into a ball under the covers in the middle of his bed. She'd fallen asleep waiting for him. He turned, closing and bolting the bedroom door. He walked over to the fireplace and reached above the mantel, taking down one of the swords he kept hanging there. He carried it to the bed and put it within reach.

A fierce protectiveness filled him. He didn't want to believe his brothers would help their father go after his mate. They all had issues with how coldly they'd been raised. He felt loyalty to his brothers and hoped they wouldn't betray him. It would be a deadly mistake if they did.

He carefully pulled back the covers and climbed in the bed behind his mate. He wrapped his body around Angel, holding her close. She murmured something in her sleep that he didn't understand but she did latch onto his arm with her hand. He examined her small fingers.

He hesitated, and then placed a kiss on her cheek before resting his head next to hers.

He'd kill anyone, regardless of their association to him, to keep her right where she belonged. That was with him.

Chapter Fifteen

Creed adjusted his sword. It would be logical for his father to assume he was out of practice with his skills fighting with one. He purposely gave that impression. But every time he'd flown to the cliffs, he'd secretly sparred with the defense teacher he'd had as a child. Delbius was his friend.

He'd always known the day may come when his father did something to make certain they battled against each other. He had no plans to lose. Especially now that Angel's future hung in the balance. His death wasn't an option. His father would make Angel his breeding vessel.

Kado entered the room alone. None of his brothers had shown for the audience with him. Creed wondered if that was a good or bad sign. They had either decided not to support their father, or he'd made a good call to allow Chaz and Fray to guard his lair to keep Angel safe in case of an attack.

From where he sat, Lord Aveoth appeared annoyed and bored at the same time. He didn't bother to mask his emotions. "Begin, Kado," he demanded.

Creed's father cleared his throat. "Did you look at my formal request and my grievances?"

"Of course I did," Aveoth stated. "I can read, and I know my duties as your lord. I'm insulted that you implied my punishment had been too lax. How dare you question it."

"Creed broke the law. He had no right to take a mate. You dishonored our traditions."

Aveoth stood and gripped his sword. "Watch it, Kado. That sounds like a challenge to my authority."

"Not at all. It is an assessment."

"I didn't ask for your opinion."

"I do believe your judgment wasn't just. I swore Creed to service for the first hundred years of his life. I did so with the intention that he'd serve this clan. I see no advantage to him taking a mate, or you allowing it. The law is clear. He is to be lashed one hundred times and encased for ten years. I ask that you follow those laws."

"Denied."

Kado looked furious. "Our laws are above reproach."

"Our laws are what I say they are. You gave Creed to this clan and that means he's mine. What part of that don't you understand? What I order him to do or what punishments I hand out to him are none of your business." Aveoth glared at his father. "I don't answer to you, nor does Creed."

"It's intent. He is to serve the greater good of our people. He hasn't done that. There are forty years of service remaining. I demand he serves it. That means he can't have a mate, and he must be appropriately punished for dishonoring my name! I know you didn't approve of your father killing women, so I believe enslaving her for forty years until his service to you is up would be a fair compromise."

"You speak of bringing dishonor to your name? You do that well enough on your own. Creed and your other sons are your only saving grace," Aveoth rumbled.

"You dare insult me?"

"Yes. I do. You come in here implying I made an error. You whine about the fact you think I've bent the laws, and yet you suggest the same thing. No mate has *ever* been enslaved for forty years. Ten years is the maximum time for punishment for this kind of offense."

"Mine was a fair suggestion. I'm willing to let her enslavement stand at ten years. Read my formal request. Everything I have asked for is reasonable."

"Bullshit. I can read between the lines. I'm not a fool," Aveoth ground out. "It's a veiled insult that you even filed it and are standing before me spouting this nonsense. I won't even begin to tell you how disgusted I am that you want permission to make Creed's mate your breeding vessel. What kind of father wishes to rape the mate of his own son and force his seed into her to birth his youngling? Then you want to expand it to forty years.

"What's next? Should she solely be for your use? You had to know your son would challenge you before he allowed it, yet you believe you can ask me to help you get away with it by encasing him first to save your ass. I *did* read what you wrote. That part was very clear. You wanted him lashed immediately and encased before he could attack you. Denied," Aveoth thundered.

"She is the reason my son cannot serve the rest of his service! It has caused dishonor in my family. I plan to disown him. I have lost a son and wish to gain another. It is only fair that *she* be that vessel. It is an appropriate way to make him suffer my loss as well."

"You are a twisted bastard," Aveoth muttered. "Please draw your sword. I dare you."

"I am not challenging you," Kado clearly stated.

"Too bad." Aveoth kept hold of his sword. "I officially deny your request and call this to a close."

"I demand a council assessment."

"I disbanded your council. Denied."

"You must realize our people won't stand for this! You are being irrational, with all respect."

Aveoth snorted. "You wouldn't know respect if it stabbed you in the heart. What did I tell you the last time you stood before me with some stupid bullshit request? This isn't a democracy. You want that? Go live with humans. They wouldn't tolerate you for long, either. Return to Europe if you don't like how I run things. I'm sure you won't like how the full-blooded clans do things. It's why you left in the first place. Your other option is to challenge me for leadership. Please do. Make my day."

Kado fisted his hands at his side. "You stand there issuing threats to me but allow Creed to blatantly disregard our laws?"

"I like him. I don't like you." Aveoth took a deep breath. "You want justification? Fine. You gave Creed to me. I decide what he does with his time, not you. His length of service is at my discretion. I went over his accomplishments. Let's talk about laws not followed, Kado. You sent your son down into our training area at the age of two. The standard is five.

227

You made him sleep there with the scouts on duty rather than allowing him to come home. That is unheard of. Our men leave the cliffs for duty when they are nearing twenty years. You and your *council* decided to ignore the law when he was fifteen and assigned Creed to serve the north post." He paused. "For *fourteen years* in a row. That's blatant cruelty. He had no ability to complete his full training or to interact with his own kind. He had no chance to learn how to handle the temptations of being around women. There are none in the north. He lost control during the ravage and mated a woman. Whose fault do you think that is? Let me answer for you—yours."

"He didn't claim a mate during his first ravage. You're wrong."

"Then he got lucky once. The odds weren't in his favor. That's how I see it."

"You're making excuses for what he did? Outrag—"

Lord Aveoth cut him off with a roar. "Enough! I'm not asking for your opinion. I'm reminding you of the laws *you* broke. You and your council conveniently forgot to add his assignment to your reports when you sent them to me." He paused. "For fourteen years straight. It was only brought to my attention when he was late to report in due to a storm. Scouts were sent out to see if he was in trouble. They were angry because he was sixteen days late before you mentioned it to them. They filed a grievance because your council put the life of one of our men at risk."

"I knew he was fine. He's my son."

Aveoth snorted. "Fine? He had to shell against a cliff to protect himself from death when the blizzard hit. He would have had to remain that way until the area thawed if they hadn't located him. No one flies alone in those conditions. That's also law. Yet you still ordered him to report to the council in person at a time you knew flying solo wasn't allowed. They had to light a fire to thaw the thick layers of ice that had formed over him. He was trapped inside his shell."

"It wouldn't have killed him."

"It was cruelty. Plain and simple. He'd gone so deep to protect himself from the icy pain of cold that they had difficulty reaching him, to let him know they were with him."

"It builds character to suffer harsh elements."

"You're a piece of work," Aveoth spat. "No one is assigned to the north for more than one year at a time, and it's always voluntary. It's a barren wasteland of boredom and would test anyone's sanity to watch nothing. It's a necessary evil since someone could attack from that direction, but it's hell." He looked at Creed. "Did you enjoy those years?"

"No." Creed glared at his father.

"I would have been stunned if you had." Aveoth released his sword, his focus on Kado. "He's owed something for the misery *you* put him through. Let's talk about justice, shall we? I'll tell you what, Kado. Why don't I assign you to the north post for fourteen years in a row? I'll call in every member of your disbanded council and assign them the same duty after your term is up. I'll make certain they are aware it's because of your grievance today, and how you accused me of being too merciful toward those who break the law."

Creed enjoyed watching his father turn ashen. He also earned a new respect for Lord Aveoth. *Well played.*

"My lord," Kado paused. "It was our job to make those assignments at the time. That was decades ago."

"You broke the law. Don't bother reminding me that he's your son, since you've already stated repeatedly that you gave him to the clan for service. That makes your claim as his father null and void, if you want to spout off about how you can tell your own children what to do as ruler of your household. I'd also have to mention he hasn't lived in your lair since the age of two." Aveoth gripped his sword again. "There's no time limit on crimes here." He glanced at four of his enforcers standing nearby. "Am I wrong?"

Kelzeb shook his head. "No, my lord."

Aveoth glared back at Kado. "Here we stand." He tilted his head. "You wanted me to be harsher in my punishments. Do you still feel that way? Or would you rather bow your head to me, tell me it was an error coming before me this morning, and withdraw your grievances?" He wasn't done. "I hear one word about how you disagree with anything I do, and I'll have you hauled back here, along with the ex-council members. I would be happy to keep the peace amongst our people by showing them ruthlessness to law breakers."

"That's blackmail," Kado hissed.

"Call it whatever the hell you want." Aveoth shrugged. "Learn, Kado. You can't win. It's why you're not reaching for your sword. You know I'd kill you. I'm stronger, smarter, and will beat you at any game you decide to play."

Kado lowered his head and bowed. "I formally withdraw all grievances." He looked up. "My request for an audience stands. I want it on record that I spoke to you, and why."

Aveoth suddenly smiled. It was cold. "I was counting on you doing just that. You still hold the belief that with enough well-placed whispers and rumors you can one day gain enough support to try to overthrow me as lord. You want proof that you stood up to me so they might give you my title. You never change, Kado. Very well. That means Creed has the right to confront you."

Aveoth backed up and waved his hand. "Proceed, Creed. This man has officially demanded to speak to me about turning your mate into his breeding vessel and removing her from your lair. He's challenged your right to keep her. It's public record."

"He broke the law, and I was told he's been confined to his lair for six months. A prisoner has no right to defend anything." Kado had a smug look on his face, and it sounded in his voice.

"What a big surprise that you'd attempt to use that ploy to avoid a fight. Your cowardice is known to everyone." Aveoth snorted. "Denied. Creed is still in service to me. We came to an understanding. You didn't see that one coming, did you? He wasn't detained to his lair—his mate was, and she's there right now. You should have asked more questions and checked your facts, Kado. Creed is in good standing with our clan. His mate begged to take his punishment...and I conceded to her wishes."

Creed walked forward and faced off against the man he had called father for all of his life. Metal scraped as he withdrew his sword from the scabbard and gripped it with both hands. He kept the tip down as he glared at Kado. He'd never think of him as a father again.

"To the death." Those were three words he'd always wanted to say—and they felt good.

"Stand down!" Kado ordered.

"Raise your sword or die a coward." Creed wasn't willing to let it go. Angel would never be in danger again from the man who'd mated his mother. "Either way, I *will* strike."

"I wasn't challenging you, Creed." Kado stumbled back a few steps.

"You wanted to take my mate, rape her, force her to become a breeder." He advanced a step and lifted his sword. "Defend yourself or bow your head so I can get a cleaner cut. Your choice."

"I'm your father! I'm ordering you to stand down!"

"You hold no authority over me." Creed refused to take his gaze off him. "Are you ordering me to stand down, Lord Aveoth?"

"No. It's your right to challenge him to the death. He did so already by attempting to steal your mate away."

"I'm *not* challenging you," his father hissed.

"You are a danger to my mate and your lack of care caused the death of my mother. Defend yourself or bow down for the removal of your head. It ends today."

Kado gripped his sword and withdrew it. Pure rage darkened his eyes. "Then you shall die, and I will remove your head!"

"Try your best. I'll even be sporting about it. You better leash that temper of yours. It never serves anyone well to take rage into the battlefield," Creed warned.

"I'll enjoy your mate's screams when I have her chained down. Your body will still be cooling on the floor when I do it. I will not be merciful to her."

"That won't happen," Kelzeb called out. "I'd challenge him first and personally return her to her pack, under my protection. He won't ever get his hands on her. I have your back, Creed. Don't allow him to distract you."

Kado shot him a contemptuous look. "Stay out of this!"

Kelzeb crossed his arms over his chest. "I'd be paying attention to *him*. I know I'm not going to have to fight you. Dead men can't lift swords."

"Get your sword ready, Kelzeb," Kado taunted. "This won't take long." He lunged, slashing the tip of his weapon at Creed.

Creed jumped back, blocking the killing blow directed at his throat. Metal clashed and sparks flew. Kado roared in rage and swung again, aiming for Creed's middle. Creed spun, blocking that one as well.

Kado leapt up, attempting to jump over him to land at his back. Creed was ready for that maneuver. He wasn't a novice. He ducked and went to one knee, spinning and throwing his blade up, preventing the killing blow from landing.

His father stumbled back and Creed kept low, throwing out a leg as he used his knee to support his weight, catching the bastard at the ankle.

Kado crashed to the floor on his back. Creed rose and backed away to give him room to stand.

"Get up. I won't finish you that fast. I'm enjoying this too much."

Kado bent his knees, one hand bracing against the floor. Creed tensed, knowing what his opponent planned.

Kado shoved hard against the floor, using the strength of his three limbs. It propelled him upward fast and it pissed Creed off. It wasn't an honorable fighting move when an opponent allowed them to recover from a fall. Kado spun when he landed, trying to nail Creed with the side with his blade.

Creed gripped the handle of his sword with both hands to make up for the strength of battling against a full-blooded Gargoyle. He met the blade with enough force that it sent Kado off-balance. Creed lunged forward and spun, throwing his arm out to the side.

Cold metal struck Kado at his neck. He hadn't shelled so it went through his skin, bone, and out the other side.

Creed froze, slightly winded.

Kado's head hit the floor first, rolling a little after it was severed. The body slumped next, dropping to its knees, then pitched forward. Blood slowly spilled from the throat.

Creed turned away, not wanting to witness the rest. He sheathed his sword and walked closer to the GarLycan lord, bending on one knee and bowing his head. "Your call, Lord Aveoth."

"Fair and just. Rise, Creed."

He knew the fight wouldn't be questioned and he wouldn't get into trouble, but it was law to get judged from their lord after a fight. He lifted his chin and stared directly into Lord Aveoth's cool gaze.

"Thank you." Creed paused. "You expected me to kill him from the moment I broke the law and took a mate, didn't you?"

"I did. I knew Kado well, unfortunately. There was no preventing it." Aveoth approached, stopping directly in front of him. It was a sign of trust. He reached out and placed his hand on Creed's shoulder. "I am sorry you had to be the one to do it, but he never would have challenged me. I knew he'd pull some stupid stunt that would force you into fighting him." He paused. "You suffered enough because of Kado. I didn't want to add to your burden but you're one of my GarLycans. This was the best way for it to end."

Creed accepted those words. "I understand. Thank you." He felt gratitude. Aveoth might have made decisions that would result in Creed being in a position to challenge Kado, but his leader was correct. Kado hadn't left him any choice. And he had to die in order to keep Angel safe.

Aveoth tightened his grip and squeezed. It was a gesture of comfort. "It's never easy but it's a necessary when we have fathers like ours. You've avenged your mother and protected your mate. Always remember that. It makes it easier to live with." His voice lowered. "I have no regrets over Lord Abotorus."

"Nor shall I over Kado."

"Go and be with your mate." He released Creed. "What do you wish done with the body?"

"Return it to my brothers. They can decide if they'd like to honor him or not with a traditional burial. He lost the right to expect that of me the day he shut me out of his lair to live elsewhere." He hesitated. "Is that too cold?"

Aveoth shook his head. "The council saw to Lord Abotorus being entombed. I held no respect for him at that time and refused to pretend otherwise. My mother wasn't in attendance, either. I'd be worried about you if wanted to do it. Sometimes our deadliest enemies are those with family bonds. Never revisit your decision. Go to your mate. It's about living now."

"Thank you." Creed bowed his head and backed away, avoiding glancing at the body or the red stains on the floor. He straightened his shoulders and took a few steps, then paused, glancing back at Kelzeb. "I'm in your debt."

"I didn't have to challenge him or fly your mate to her pack. You owe me nothing, Creed. Just be happy. It's what all of us want."

Creed faced forward, leaving the room. His brothers might seek vengeance. It was doubtful though. It was on record that Kado had wanted to enslave his mate, and Lord Aveoth had deemed the fight fair and just. No one would believe he'd had a choice in the matter. To defend a mate was honorable. Kado had set it all in motion by his own actions.

He made it to the door of his lair and addressed Fray. "Any trouble?"

"No. I'll fly out and tell Chaz we're off duty. He was watching your ledge in case they tried to get at her that way."

"I appreciate it. I am in your debt."

"No, you aren't." Fray grinned. "Kelzeb offered us a week off to do this little babysitting job. It was the easiest gig he's had us do in a while. Last week we had to take out a nest of Vampires. Two masters banded together, thinking they were hot shit and above reproach since they'd amassed over sixty suckheads under their control. They were blatant enough to start drawing attention. That was some intense shit. I had to burn my favorite duster and boots." He glanced down. "I hate breaking new ones in but I couldn't get the damn ash and blood out of the old ones. Do you get much Vampire action guarding the Lycan village?"

"No. They avoid going that far out."

"Sounds like a vacation every day of the year." Fray paused, glancing down him, then back up. "Are you okay?"

"Yes."

"I smell the blood, and figured you'd have to take out your old man. I'm sorry. Not everyone got as lucky as Chaz and I."

"I don't understand."

"Our father is a full-blood but he's not like the others. He removed the stick from his ass and is pretty modern. He can't stand most of the other Gargoyles. Of course, he's practically a baby compared to the ones who founded and built our home inside the cliffs."

"You're GarLycan?"

"I am. Mom was a Lycan."

"Was?"

"She wasn't one of the doves who live here."

"Doves?"

237

"You know. Mates who stay at home. They perch in our nests. Mom wanted to fight at Dad's side, and he let her walk all over him." He smiled. "They were crazy about each other." His features sobered. "He couldn't tell her no about anything, including that. They were ambushed twelve years ago. They were supposed to wait for us to meet them outside of the nest but shit turned sour before we arrived. Mom was killed."

"I'm sorry."

"Thanks. It's why Chaz and I always take on suckheads. That's what killed her. They drained her fucking dry before Dad could get to her. I heard you lost your mother too."

"Yes. It was eleven years ago."

"Now you have a mate. Enjoy it. She seems nice, and man, she knows how to fight. I was impressed seeing her take on that Lycan. She can handle herself for a human."

"Thank you. But I hope she never has to fight again."

Fray nodded. "Amen to that, brother. I'll get Chaz."

Creed watched the other man walk away and then entered his lair.

He bolted the door behind him, going straight to Angel. She waited inside the bedroom, sitting on his couch with a fire blazing. She held an open book in her hands. Happiness sparked in her entire expression when she saw him.

"How did it go?" Angel closed the book and stood, rushing toward him. She'd been worried ever since he'd left. "What happened?"

"Lord Aveoth denied everything my father requested." He removed his sword, laying it flat on the mantel, and then unbuckled the belt securing the sheath, resting it against the wall. He pulled her into his arms.

"Your dad is a tool but don't let him get to you."

"He's dead."

She jerked her head up, staring at him. Shock tore through her. "What?"

"I had to challenge him, Angel. He would have kept coming after you."

His words hit her hard. "Oh my God."

"It's okay."

"You killed your dad because of me?" She clutched at him, horrified and heartbroken at the same time. "I'm so sorry!"

"He left me with no choice. Don't apologize."

"You're going to resent me." It was her worst fear coming true.

Creed scowled. "Never."

"You had to kill your *dad* over me!"

"It wasn't just about you. He is the reason my mother died. It was just a matter of time before I took his life or he tried to take mine."

She wanted to believe that. She just couldn't.

Creed must have seen something in her features because he leaned in, getting a better grip on her.

"Listen to me. He was not a good man, Angel. He forced me into this position, and challenging him was the only option left. I refused to live with the worry of what he'd do next to make me miserable. He's done it all my life. I will admit you were part of the motivation that drove me into removing his head today, but it was inevitable. I'm relieved that it's over with and done. Do you understand?"

She nodded. "How are you holding up?"

His expression cleared of all emotion. "I'm at peace with it."

"He was your father, Creed. This has to hurt."

He hesitated but finally spoke. "That would imply we had a bond that didn't exist. He impregnated my mother but he was never a father. Would you mourn the man you knew as a small child that was once your father?"

"I barely remember him, Creed. But no, I wouldn't."

"My conception wasn't planned. I was a result of the ravage and my mother going into heat at the same time. She admitted she was lonely and purposely got pregnant. She wanted me desperately, but he flew into a rage once he realized how far the pregnancy had progressed before he'd noticed. It was too late to force her to end it. That's why he resigned me to a hundred years of service to the clan. He didn't want to be bothered by me. He took me from my mother when I was two years old to live with the scouts to begin my training. I was raised by the men who taught me how to fight and fly. He even limited the visits my mother was allowed. I believe it's part of the reason he sent me away from the cliffs on a long assignment when I was too young to leave. He hated the sight of me and the way my mother kept trying to be a part of my life. She loved me very much, and she always let me know it."

It broke her heart for him. "I'm so sorry."

"I do not mourn him, Angel. He was more enemy than family."

240

She buried her face against his chest, clinging to him. "What can I do to help you?"

He rested his chin on the top of her head. "I would enjoy it if you'd share my bath."

She smiled and eased her hold on him. "I can do that."

"That would cheer my mood." He ran his hands down to her ass, massaging both cheeks. "Very much so."

She chuckled. "Me too."

He backed off and released her. "I'll run the water."

"I'll be there in a few minutes." She let him go and watched him disappear into the bathroom.

Regardless of what he said, Angel was sure it must bother him that he'd had to kill his own father. To see someone beheaded would traumatize anyone, but Creed had been holding that sword.

She walked to the mantel and ignored how her hands trembled when she lifted the sword. It was heavier than it looked. There was surprisingly only a little blood on it.

She carefully carried it by the handle into the kitchen and angled the blade across the sink. He'd protected her, and she wanted to do the same for him. She turned on the water and began to clean away the blood. Red swirled in the sink before it drained away. Then she carefully dried it. Angel hurried into the bedroom with a wet dish towel to clean where the blade had touched the wood.

"Angel?"

"I'll be there soon. Go ahead and get in."

Making certain all the blood traces were gone, she turned, jogging back into the kitchen. It only took a few minutes to rinse out the dishtowel.

Finally, she went to her mate.

He'd done the difficult thing to protect her from his father. He might have had a lot of reasons to kill him, but the timing had been her fault. She forced a smile to her lips and began to remove his borrowed shirt she wore. Creed had already climbed into the tub, the water chest high.

He smiled back at her, his gaze lingering over her body as he took her in. "You're so beautiful."

"I love you too." She planned to seduce him, and keep him distracted from thoughts of what he'd had to do to protect her.

Chapter Sixteen

It stunned Creed to see his eldest brother at the cliffs. Neb was sent on a lot of missions for the clan, traveling all over the place.

Pure rage simmered in his brother's eyes. It was a given that word had traveled of Kado's death.

Creed stiffened, wishing he wore his sword. It remained in the bedroom. "Give me a few moments to prepare. Can we fight in one of the training rooms? My mate can't leave my home and I don't want her harmed."

"I didn't come here to challenge you, Creed."

He glanced down his brother's uniform. "You're in battle gear."

"I heard what happened and came right here from my assignment. I didn't take time to change or to stop at my home. May I enter?" His brother glanced away, looking down the corridors, then back at him. "I'd rather talk to you in private. I have no intentions of harming your mate or starting shit with you."

Creed opened the door wider and stepped back. "You're welcome in my home."

Neb strode forward. Creed closed and barred the door. He followed him inside and spotted Angel coming down the hallway. He moved fast to get between her and Neb. He motioned for her to stop and stay back. He hated the worry he identified in her look and the way she stared at his brother.

Neb peered back at her and slightly bowed. "You must be Angel. I am Creed's eldest brother, Nebulas. You may call me Neb. Welcome to our family, as fucked up as it is." He turned to face Creed. "Your mate is beautiful but I had faith that she would be. She's more delicate than I imagined but I approve of your choice."

"It's not a requirement to me."

Neb chuckled. "I am glad to hear it." He sobered. "So father finally pushed you too far. I don't blame you for what happened. I would have taken him out eleven years ago but mother made the rest of us swear to never kill him. You were her only son she spared from making that promise...but he was harshest with you. She was a realist, and knew the day would come when he forced you into a challenge. How are you holding up? Tell me you aren't grieving that son of a bitch."

"I'm at peace."

Neb nodded. "Good. You should be." He turned his head, studying Angel. "I don't know if you met our father but if anyone deserved to die, it was him." He looked back at Creed. "I'm at peace with his death. I wanted you to know we're good."

"What about our brothers?"

"I haven't spoken to them yet. I came directly to you. I know they are at the cliffs. I'll track them down next and have a talk with them but I don't believe either will hold a grudge. He ordered all three of us to come yesterday when he learned of you taking a mate." He paused. "I'm just sorry it took me so long to get here. I had orders to locate a nest last night and it couldn't be put off. They had stolen a group of Lycan kids we needed to retrieve."

"Why would Vampires do that?" Angel came closer, pressing up against Creed's side, staring at his brother.

"The blood bastards think it's amusing to make the boys fight to the death, and children are easier for them to snatch while they are off pack lands. The ones taken were going to movies or visiting malls. We've had a string of kidnappings in various states lately. It's like a new sick sport for them, and it's pissing us off. They've been taking them in the ten- to fourteen-year range. Old enough to shift but young enough to be overpowered and stolen."

"Their guardians weren't able to track the missing youths?" Creed frowned. He hadn't heard anything about it.

"There are no guardians on the Lycan packs who've been targeted so far. They've contacted Lord Aveoth, begging for assistance. We've been working with some of the VampLycans on finding the nests responsible. Our neighbors fear those blood bastards might try to grab pack women to breed next, so they got involved. Nobody wants a repeat of the past or kids dying. The shit we've seen is pretty bad."

It alarmed Creed. He wondered if Lord Aveoth had already sent another guardian to protect the Henita pack. "Do you have a phone?"

Neb withdrew one from his back pocket and offered it to him.

"Give it to me." Angel held out her hand. "I have my parents' number memorized. I'll warn them." She was thinking the same thing he was. The Lycan kids in her pack could be in danger.

Creed passed it to her and watched her dial. She pressed it up to her ear and he could hear it ring twice before a woman answered. Angel held still, probably guessing he and his brother could overhear the conversation. She'd been raised by a Lycan pack. They all had excellent hearing.

"Hi, Mom."

"You made it home safe? I worried when I tried to call you and you didn't answer your cell last night. It's not like you, but I figured you had to be exhausted after not sleeping well, having to travel home, and then go to work."

"Sorry. Listen, did a new guardian show up?"

"Not that I've heard. Where is Creed? Isn't he up on the mountain?"

"No. Look, I'll call you again later and fill you in, but I need you to know something. Some Vampires have been kidnapping young Lycans and making them fight to the death. Creed isn't there right now to protect our pack. Gather everyone and put them on alert. Have them on watch at night and keep the young ones safe. Do you understand?"

"Is that happening to the Washington packs? I thought you didn't talk to them. Did Creed tell you he was leaving here? Why? What's going on?"

Angel met Creed's eyes, and then glanced at his brother. "Do you mind if I borrow your phone for a few minutes?"

"Go ahead."

She looked back at Creed.

"Tell her everything," he urged.

"Mind if I do this in the bedroom?"

He shook his head. "Go, Angel. We'll be here."

Angel disappeared down the hallway and closed his bedroom door.

Creed sighed and addressed his brother. "Her parents haven't been told yet that we're mated. I just left without speaking to the elders where I was guardian, and we were brought straight here. She needed to warn her pack."

Emotion flashed in Neb's eyes. "Father didn't tell me much when he called. She's human, not Lycan, and the only human associated with the pack you protect is the child you once found in the woods. That's her? The little girl?"

"She grew up."

Neb grinned. "No shit. Do you have anything to drink around here? I'd love to hear this story."

Creed smiled. "Have a seat."

Neb removed his weapons, stacking them on the counter. "I'm all ears."

Angel walked over to the fireplace and took a seat on the couch. She was nervous as she tried to think of the right words to say. "Um, can you sit down, Mom?"

"What is going on, Angel?"

"Is Dad with you?"

"No. He's training some of the youth this morning."

"Okay. Well, there's something I didn't tell you. You know how the ravage makes GarLycans emotional?"

"Yes."

"Well, I pushed Creed, and he kind of lost control. It was totally my fault. He bit me."

Silence over the phone was the only response.

"I'm at the cliffs. We were ordered to come here after their lord discovered we mated. I'm fine, and happy to be Creed's mate. We didn't get permission first so that was kind of a no-no." She wasn't about to explain everything. It would just alarm her mother more. "Long story short, we're together and happy. I'm just going to be here for a few months."

"Oh shit," her mother gasped.

"It's *fine*," Angel rushed. "New mates stay at the cliffs." That was possibly true. The enforcers who'd found her said something about how they thought all men going through the ravage should come home to do it. "Creed's home is really nice, and I'm truly happy. It's just that right now, he's not up on the mountain to protect the pack. You need to gather the pack and tell them about the Vampire attacks on kids. They're supposedly going after kids as young as ten, okay? Keep them out of human towns and close. Creed and I just found out, and I had to call to let you know."

"Why didn't you say something about being his mate when he brought you home?"

"I didn't want you to freak out and we didn't know how Creed's people were going to react. It's all fine now, I swear. I'm good. I love Creed. You know that."

"How is he responding to having you for a mate?"

"Really great."

"He isn't furious or upset?"

"No." Angel gripped the phone tighter. "I swear. I know what you're probably thinking. I would have assumed he'd be furious but that's not the case. He's been so sweet and wonderful with me." She lowered her voice. "We've even talked about having a baby. We're leaving it to nature. He loves me too."

"He said that?"

Angel smiled and relaxed. "He shows me every time he touches and looks at me, Mom. He's still a GarLycan. It's going to take some time for him to verbally express how he feels. But he makes me happy."

"Your father is going to want to go there. So do I."

"Right now, you need to protect the pack. Creed and I will be returning there as soon as Lord Aveoth says we can go."

"Why are they keeping you? Why can't you come home now?"

"New-mate thing." Her mother would freak out if she told her they were being punished. Then she remembered the Lycan at the airport. "I'm putting off a scent that new mates get. It's complicated, but I'd drive unmated Lycan men insane. I smell like I'm in heat big time."

"Are you safe from other GarLycans?"

"Yes. Creed would never allow anyone to hurt me. You know that, Mom. He's my mate. I will call you tomorrow, okay? This phone belongs to Creed's brother."

"Where's your phone?"

She wasn't sure where her things were. She hadn't seen them since they'd entered GarLycan territory. "I forgot to charge it," she lied. "I'll do that soon."

"You call tomorrow."

"I will. I love you and Dad. Tell him I'm fine and happy. I promise. And tell the elders and alpha *now* that the kids are in danger."

"We'll take care of the pack. We're not helpless without a guardian."

"I know, but I'm also aware that we've grown to depend on Creed a lot to keep us safe at night."

"That is true."

"I love you, Mom."

"I love you too."

Angel ended the call and stood, crossed the room, and opened the bedroom door. The sound of two men laughing made her smile. It seemed at least one of Creed's brothers accepted that he'd mated her, or at least didn't mind. She walked into the living space to find both of them sitting on the couch holding beers in hand. Creed patted the couch and she went to him, taking a seat. She reached over his lap to give his brother the borrowed phone back.

"Did it go well?" Creed appeared worried.

"My parents know how I've always felt about you. Dad wasn't home but my mom will tell him. I'm sure they'll be happy once the shock wears off. She's also going to gather the pack to warn them about kids being taken. They'll probably assign perimeters for the pack to patrol tonight until the danger passes or we go back there."

"I have some time free. I finished my last assignment and am due time off." Neb sipped his beer. "I could cover being the guardian for that pack during my vacation. You said Lord Aveoth gave her six months' confinement? I'll talk to Kelzeb. I'm sure he'll assign someone there when I need to return to duty, if asked."

"I'd appreciate that." Creed put his arm around Angel, pulling her closer. "I've grown to care about those Lycans."

"I can be there by tomorrow night, and that will give me time to speak to our brothers before I leave."

"Thank you." Angel was touched. "That's really nice of you."

"Watching over a quiet area will be a good change of pace." Neb grinned. "I've seen too much death over the past few years. The blood bastards have kept me pretty busy, between thinking it was cool to grow huge nests they couldn't keep under control and now going after Lycan kids."

"Thank you," Creed rasped. "I'll sleep better at night knowing you're looking out for Angel's family and friends. The elders are a bit talkative but I just think of something else while they're speaking to me. They are going to want to go over what they expect from you as their guardian. Just nod every so often."

Neb shook his head. "Only you would do that, brother. You always did have the patience of a saint. I just plan to drive in, tell them I'm there, and give them my number to call if I'm needed. Then I'll stalk their air until morning. Are there any hot bitches who have a curiosity about GarLycans?"

"Most of them are mated, and I avoided the rest," Creed confessed, glancing at Angel.

"Sorry." Neb winced. "I didn't mean to bring up anything taboo."

"I avoided all the women who might have shown an interest in me." Creed rubbed Angel's back. "I couldn't have the only one I wanted. There's nothing to hide. I never took any of her pack to my bed."

Angel knew that. She'd have heard if Creed had taken a lover. Her parents wouldn't have told her but her friends would have. It made her love him even more. "I love you so much for that."

"I couldn't hurt you that way."

Neb cleared his throat. "So where did you go to find company? I'd like to know where I can pick up a woman."

Creed looked at his brother. "I didn't."

Neb gaped at him. "Weren't you there for like twenty-five years?"

"Closer to three decades."

"Shit." Neb glanced between them, finally holding Angel's eyes. "And you? Did you ever date anyone from the pack?"

She shook her head. "Creed had rejected my offer to be his mate right after I turned legal age. I dated one guy from another pack. It didn't make me forget him or how much I loved him, so that's when I moved away."

"You two are breaking my heart," Neb sighed. "Fuck, I hate our father all over again for a new reason. You could have mated her back then if he hadn't sworn you to a hundred years of service. Fucking bastard. It worked out though. You're together now."

Angel nodded. "And we'll never be apart."

"I can drink to that." Neb tipped his beer bottle and finished it off. "I'm going to go look for our brothers, make sure their heads aren't up their asses about what you had to do, and then I'll get assigned to be a guardian." He stood.

Creed let Angel go and got to his feet. He hesitated but then hugged his brother, who embraced him back. "Thank you."

"For what? Not being anything like our father? I try damn hard not to be. May he burn in hell, if there is such a place. He had it coming."

Angel watched as Neb gathered his weapons, strapped them on, and then Creed escorted him out. Her mate returned with a smile on his face and she walked to him.

"I'm so glad that went well," she confessed.

"I don't think my other brothers will be a problem. If they are, I'll deal with them. I have Neb's support. They'll heed his words when he speaks to them. All of us looked up to him more so than our father. He was the one who tried to look out for us."

"How did he look out for you?"

"He used to sneak away to visit even when I was stuck at the north border. He brought me presents to help occupy my time and letters from our mother. Neb is the one who brought my other brothers to your territory right after I was assigned to be guardian there. The bed I mated you in was actually a gift from Neb, and he had my other brothers help him fly it to me." He grinned. "He said I should have a comfortable place to sleep since he knows guardians usually don't end up with the best accommodations."

"I'm glad you had that, Creed."

"It would have caused him trouble if our father had found out he'd spent time with us. Neb did it anyway. He wanted us brothers to be close, despite our father's attempts to keep us apart."

"Why would your dad want that? Siblings should be close."

"My guess? He wanted our loyalty to remain with him and not to each other. He probably feared we'd stand together against him. He was such a cold son of a bitch."

It hurt her, imagining his childhood, but it helped knowing he'd had Neb. She liked his older brother. "Our kids will be close."

Creed reached up and cupped her face with both his hands. "They will be loved by their mother and father. I will encourage them to feel emotions and allow you to hug and kiss them so they know how important they are to us."

"You're going to make an amazing father."

Doubt clouded his eyes and she hated to see it. He didn't protest but the silence spoke for him.

"You'll be hugging and kissing on our babies when they're born. I know that. even if you're not so sure yet."

"I can't even imagine."

"You gave an abused, frightened child to Lycans. I didn't know how great my life could become until you gifted me with a loving family. It's your turn to be saved by me."

He smiled. "I look forward to it."

Chapter Seventeen

They were eating in the kitchen a few hours later when the pounding on the door jolted them both.

Creed rose, grabbed Angel's arm, and hurried her into the bedroom. "Stay here," he ordered. "Bolt the door behind me." He grabbed the sword next to the bed, strode to the fireplace, and took down the second one.

"Wait!" Angel grabbed his arm. "Do you have more weapons?"

He nodded. "In the wardrobe."

She let him go. "Do you know who's out there?"

"No, but I'll find out. Probably my brothers. I'll assume they didn't agree with Neb and have a problem with my challenging our father to the death."

The pounding grew louder, and he knew time was up. They'd break in the door soon, and he wanted to battle them in the corridor instead of his home. "Bolt the door."

He rushed into the living room, wishing he had his belt on to sheathe his swords. He had to set one against the wall in order to unlock the door and jerked it open. It hit the wall as he grabbed the sword so he had them both in hand. A rumble came from him as three men in the hallway leapt backward.

Creed recognized each face.

He should have predicted that the surviving council members would have a problem with him killing one of them. He tensed and lowered his weapons, keeping the blades down. "Did you come to challenge me? I'll assume that's why you're beating on my door. When and which of you shall I fight?"

Domb pulled his sword—but so did Milgo and Lisser. The three Gargoyles spaced each other by four feet, leaving Creed trapped with only the open doorway at his back. They obviously meant to attack him.

"You have no honor if you do this," Creed pointed out. "You want to challenge me? Do it fairly one on one. Issue a time and I'll meet you in court. All challenges are to be performed before Lord Aveoth for his ruling. You know this."

Domb sneered. "We don't acknowledge him as our lord."

Creed gripped his weapons tighter, taking a defensive stance. The bastards had him outnumbered three to one. They were bad odds. "Cowards," he accused.

"Executioners," Milgo argued coldly. "You murdered a council member. We sentence you to death."

"Lord Aveoth will kill you for this." Creed had learned enough about his leader to know he wouldn't allow them to get away with slaughtering one of the clan. He glared at Domb. "So will Kelzeb. Isn't he your son?"

"I will disown him," Domb spat.

"They both are plotting to kill us anyway." Lisser began to slightly shell. "We've been stripped of power, and Kado's death was methodically orchestrated."

"That's a lie. Have the three of you lost your sanity? I mated a human and my father tried to have me encased for it and demanded that she be enslaved as his breeder. No man would allow that to go unchallenged." Creed slightly shelled his skin. "At least have the honor to come at me single file."

Lisser stepped back a few feet, silently agreeing by lowering his weapon.

Domb swung his sword and lunged forward. So did Milgo.

Creed was glad he'd been taught to use double swords when worried about an attack. It was tempting to completely shell. They wouldn't be able to kill him, but he wouldn't be able to move or protect his mate if he did. That wasn't an option.

Metal clashed as he kept Domb back and saved his neck from Milgo taking a swipe at it.

"What the fuck?"

The voice was a familiar one to Creed, but he couldn't spare a glance down the corridor to see which one of his brother's spoke since they sounded alike.

"We've got your back!" another voice shouted, again familiar.

Milgo spun, moving off. That left Creed fighting Domb. The Gargoyle was a bit stronger but Creed was desperate to protect the door and his mate inside. Adrenaline surged through his body and he found extra strength. He blocked another blow and was able to position himself enough to see what was going on around him.

His two brothers were taking on Milgo and Lisser. No matter how they felt about him challenging their father, he was grateful that they were fighting *with* him rather than against him.

Domb rumbled deeply, leapt back, and shot a glare at the other fighting men. He curled his lip before he took another swing with his sword at Creed.

He blocked the blade aimed at his chest. He could see Domb was becoming frustrated when Creed was able to use his swords to avoid taking direct hits. The Gargoyle unshelled his body to be able to move faster. It gave him an advantage but also made him more vulnerable to injuries his harder skin would have deflected.

Creed took advantage and managed to land a strike on Domb's shoulder. Blood poured down his arm, soaking his shirt where it had sliced open. The Gargoyle roared from the pain and stumbled back. He shelled fast and hard, his skin turning gray.

Creed didn't allow him to recover, instead focusing on disarming the bastard. It took three swings of his swords to send Domb's flying from his hand.

"Submit," Creed snarled.

Domb lunged at him. He couldn't move too fast with his body in that dark gray state. Creed dropped his swords and spun, twisted out of the way, and threw out a leg. The Gargoyle tripped and crashed into the floor. Creed watched as the man had to soften his skin enough to get up. Swords clashed nearby but he didn't look away from the pissed-off ex-council member, even when someone screamed in pain.

Domb spun and held a dagger in his hand. He lunged, attempting to stab Creed in the throat. He missed making a direct hit, but pain lanced the side of Creed's neck.

Domb had to stay unshelled to be able to move fast, and Creed took advantage by letting his claws loose and punching them into his opponent's chest.

The Gargoyle roared from the pain and jerked back, but then attempted to plunge the dagger into Creed's face, going for his eye.

Creed managed to dodge and stabbed out with his claws again, scoring a direct hit to Domb's exposed throat. Protective instincts over his mate and rage had him twisting his wrist viciously before he even gave it thought. Blood sprayed, and he used his other hand to stab into his enemy's throat too, slashing.

Domb dropped and Creed jumped back.

Shouts and pounding boots sounded as Creed panted, his fingers soaked with blood. He watched as Domb struggled to breathe, choking on his own blood. Most of his throat had been destroyed. Creed expected the man to shell in an attempt to save his own life. It would stop the bleeding. He'd eventually heal, but he'd have to remain in a hard shell for months to survive that much damage.

He didn't.

"Shit!"

Creed glanced to his side when Duster stepped next to him. The scout had others with him, who also crowded around the downed ex-council member. They looked as if they'd just come off shift, since all four of them wore their uniforms. Duster pulled out his cell phone, making a call. Creed heard him informing someone, probably Lord Aveoth or Kelzeb, that there was a problem and the location.

"Shell," Creed ordered Domb. "You'll die otherwise."

Domb managed to lift his gaze from where he was on his knees a few feet away. A look of hatred blazed from the bastard's cold eyes.

Duster ended the call. "What happened?"

"They came to my home and planned to execute me." Creed finally glanced back to take in the rest of the corridor. It came as a shock to see the other two council members dead on the floor. His two brothers were alive but Glacier had a cut on his right cheek and cradled his bleeding arm. His other brother appeared fine but angry.

"Thank you." Creed appreciated that they'd come to his defense.

"You're our brother." Glacier shrugged. "Neb sent us both to let you know we're fine with what happened with Kado. We'll talk about that later, though."

Duster moved and Creed watched as the scout knelt, staring at Domb. His voice was soft as he spoke. "You're bleeding out. Shell. That's an order."

Domb removed one of his hands. Blood spread down his chest faster when he did. He flipped the scout off and his mouth moved. No sound came but Creed could read the "fuck you" clear enough. Domb collapsed to his side on the floor. He gasped and choked but stayed down.

Duster rose up and put his hand on his sword. "I should end it faster for him. That's a bad way to go and he seems hell-bent on dying."

"Don't bother," Glacier grumbled. "We came upon him and the other council member unfairly attacking our baby brother. Two on one is cowardice. A merciful death goes to those who have honor. Let the prick choke to death."

Braze, the scout to Creed's right, drew his sword. "He probably doesn't want to live now that the other council members are dead. I'll do it."

Duster motioned him back. "Kelzeb is on his way right now. We'll let him decide. It's his father, after all."

Domb became utterly quiet as the minutes passed. Kelzeb and Lord Aveoth arrived. Creed retreated to his open door and stayed there, guarding it. He watched as Kelzeb knelt next to Domb and checked on his father. He lowered his head and closed his eyes.

Lord Aveoth grasped his friend and lead enforcer's shoulder. His words came out low but they carried. "Is he dead?"

Kelzeb rose up and opened his eyes. "Yes." He glanced around at the bodies on the floor. "What happened?"

"They came to execute me." Creed held his gaze. "Your father and Milgo drew their weapons, refused to go to court with me to settle the matter, and attacked. Lisser hung back. My brothers arrived and evened out the odds. I told Domb to shell when I tore open his throat but he refused."

"I told him to shell as well," Duster sighed. "He refused me as well."

Lord Aveoth's eyes flashed sliver. "They came to execute you?"

Creed nodded. "They didn't want to challenge me in your court. They stated they didn't acknowledge you as their lord. It was payback for my father's death. I would have been killed if Glacier and Pest hadn't arrived when they did."

"Goddamn it." Lord Aveoth lifted his hand and ran it though his hair. "Why am I not surprised that they'd pull this shit?" He dropped his arm to his side. "I'm glad you're fine." He spared looks to Creed's brothers, giving them a slight nod. "Good job."

Kelzeb looked a little shaken up but he approached Creed and stopped a few feet in front of him. "I apologize. I should have posted guards at your door, but I didn't think they'd be stupid enough to seek vengeance for Kado's death."

Creed relaxed slightly, grateful the lead enforcer wasn't angry with him for killing his father. "It's not your fault. I don't understand why Domb wouldn't shell."

"He always was a stubborn bastard. His council meant more to him than anyone else ever did. He lost them all, and I'm sure it stung his pride that a lowly GarLycan took him in a fight. You did what you had to." He turned and spoke to Lord Aveoth. "I need to go to my mother. I want her to hear the news from me that her mate is dead."

"Go. Be with her. We can handle this." Lord Aveoth began to give the scouts orders to remove the bodies. He finally gave Creed his attention. "We have this. Go into your home with your mate." He turned to Creed's brothers. "You came to talk to him. Do it."

Glacier didn't budge. "We're all good?"

Lord Aveoth actually smiled. "I deem your actions appropriate. There will be no punishment or reprimands for what happened here. The ex-council members attempted to murder Creed. It was prevented. Spend time with your brother."

Creed backed into his home and his brothers followed. He spun, walking fast to his bedroom door. "Angel? It's fine. Open the door."

She unbolted the door and threw it open. He had to grin at seeing his mate. She held a short blade in one hand, as if ready to fight. He stepped inside and carefully took it from her, placing it on the nearest surface.

"Are you okay? I heard the fighting and someone screamed." She clung to his waist, burying her face against his chest. "I was so scared for you."

He hugged her tight. "I'm fine. My other brothers are here. They showed up and saved me."

She looked up at him. "Are they mad about your father?"

He wasn't sure. "Let's go find out."

Angel was nervous as Creed led her into the living room. Two men waited. One was injured and bleeding. She would have known they were related to her mate by looks alone. Their features were enough like Creed's and they had the same body types. Tall and muscular. She let go of Creed's hand and went into the kitchen, wetting a dish towel before striding up to the bleeding one. "Sit."

He arched a black eyebrow but grinned. "Okay." He took a seat on a barstool.

She inched forward and began to dab the cloth at his face to clean away the blood. The injury had already stopped bleeding and begun to heal. She turned her attention to his arm next. It looked as if he'd been cut across his forearm. It still bled a little. "I'll get the first-aid kit." She turned to Creed. "Do we have one?"

Creed snagged her around the waist from behind and dragged her a few feet back. "He'll be fine."

"But he's hurt and he's your brother." She flashed him a frown.

"His name is Glacier. I'm Pest."

She stared up at the other brother. He had black hair and dark eyes. It was hard to tell their color. Not black but they reminded her of heavy thunderclouds. "Pest?"

He grinned. "Blame Neb for that handle they stuck me with."

"He has an actual name but he gets pissed when we use it."

She stared back at Glacier. He had black hair too, his features the most like Creed's. They could have been almost twins except his eyes were a very lively light blue.

"Shut it," Pest warned.

Creed pulled her closer against the front of him and bent his head. "Tempest," he whispered.

Pest shot him a dirty look. "I hate that name. It sounds like a girl's." His expression softened when he gazed at Angel. "I got teased, and still do when anyone learns my name."

She shook her head. "You think Pest is better?"

He shrugged and took a seat on a barstool next to Glacier. "I can be one. It at least fits me."

"You can also be a bit girly," Glacier replied.

Pest punched him on his injured arm.

"Ouch!"

"Who's whining now?" Pest grinned. "You don't see me bleeding, do you? How in the hell did you let your guard down twice?"

"The bastard was just standing there so I was watching you fight. He got in a sneak attack with a dagger before I could react. He was aiming for my neck but I flinched and he got my face instead." Glacier took the wet dish towel and wrapped it around his arm. "*This* happened when I opened myself up so he'd take a swing at me. I blocked it with my arm and was able to take his head."

Angel glanced up at Creed, confused and alarmed.

"The three council members decided to punish me for killing our father. They came to kill me. All three of them are dead instead."

She knew the blood drained out of her face. "Are you in trouble?"

"No. It was justifiable. Lord Aveoth arrived with Kelzeb. It's fine."

"We saved our baby brother's ass." Pest chuckled. "He owes us now. I'm hungry. Is your mate a good cook? A nice meal will make us even."

Creed let her go and growled at his brother. "My mate isn't cooking for you, but I will."

"You haven't formally introduced us but it's not necessary." Glacier winked at her. "You're Angel. It's nice to meet you."

Pest leaned back in his chair to appraise her with his eyes. "You're smaller than I expected, but it's not a shock that our baby brother ended up with a human. We heard about you last night from the dickhead. He was ranting and raging about it."

Glacier snorted. "The dickhead, otherwise known as our father." He turned to watch Creed move around the kitchen. "We tried like hell to talk him out of pulling his bullshit this morning, but he wouldn't listen. Big shocker, right? We're just the idiots our mother birthed."

"Big mistakes, and his precious Gargoyle sperm wasted," Pest muttered. "Every one of us."

"He would have killed us in our cradles if he'd only known how weak and disappointing we'd turn out to be," Glacier added. "Man, I'm not going to miss him. Did you really think we'd be ass-hurt over you taking him out, Creed? Come on. The only reason we hadn't challenged the bastard ourselves was because Mom made us swear to let him keep breathing."

Angel blinked back tears. It broke her heart to hear what they were saying and imagining growing up with Kado as a father. She'd had two amazing parents that Creed had given her. He'd rescued her from that very kind of upbringing.

"You didn't show up at court." Creed paused at the open fridge. "I hoped that meant you weren't on his side." He took out wrapped meat and carried it to the counter.

"We didn't go because we planned to protect Angel. Dickhead and those idiots we just killed were always thick as thieves." Pest sighed. "We kept an eye on his only friends in case he decided to have his council grab your mate. He was paranoid and thought Lord Aveoth had it out for him. They never left their homes, though. I was stationed in the hallway watching their doors and Glacier watched their part of the cliff."

"Which Lord Aveoth probably did," Glacier added. "He's smart, and he had to know what a shit our father was. Only a moron would trust the council. Plus, his new mate is half human and half VampLycan. No way would our lord hand over any woman to be a breeder to any of them after the stunt they pulled when he made the announcement. I heard how pissed he was."

Creed fried the meat in a pan while Angel studied the two brothers. Glacier caught her staring at him and smiled.

"I look a lot like your mate, don't I?"

She nodded. "It's a little eerie, actually. Your eyes are different, though. I've never seen anything like them."

"Don't get him started." Pest chuckled. "He'll tell you all about how we got stuck with our names."

"I'm interested in hearing that," she admitted.

Glacier grinned. "The dickhead couldn't be bothered with us as infants. That meant Mom got to name us. Unlike humans, we aren't born and instantly given names. It happens days afterward. Nebulas has some purple in his eyes, and Mom said she named him since she'd read books on the subject from some eighteen-hundreds astronomer guy. He described things he believed were in outer space so Neb got stuck with that name. I was born next. My eyes reminded her of glaciers. My father had flown her to the cliffs during winter so she saw plenty of them. They mostly traveled over the ocean to reach here and stayed on one during the day for him to rest." He pointed to Pest. "Do you want to tell her, or shall I?"

"I got stuck with Tempest because it means violent windstorm. Want to guess what hit when she was in labor with me, and lasted for days? It was so bad she could hear it in her bedroom." He sighed. "She couldn't pick something cool like Storm. Nope. Tempest."

"He also howled a lot," Glacier teased. "Loudest damn infant ever. Maybe she mistook him for a girl with all that crying he did."

Pest growled and made a fist. "Want me to punch your arm again?"

Creed put food on two plates and set them on the counter in front of his brothers. "Eat and stop fighting."

"Just meat? No side dishes?" Pest scowled. "That's a shitty thank you. I killed someone and don't even rate mashed potatoes?"

"I wasn't expecting company." Creed crossed his arms. "Take it or leave it."

"Silverware would be nice." Pest arched an eyebrow.

Creed spun away to get them.

"You brothers talk so differently. Why?" Angel had noticed.

"Our baby brother was raised with scouts, then sent to the barren zone for a lot of years where there was no one to talk to, and he's not exactly got a shit-ton of friends." Glacier grimaced. "Dickhead made sure he was a loner. Creed was stuck playing the enslaved son while the rest of us got the hell out of dodge."

"That being here—or should we say, away from our father." Pest snorted. "So, baby bro there is way more formal than we are and kind of a stick in the mud. We're hoping you loosen him up a bit."

It made sense to her. "What about Creed's name? How did your mother pick it?" Angel was curious.

It was Glacier who answered. "Mom was going through religious books, reading all about different ones while she was pregnant with him. The dickhead was making her life a living hell at the time because he was furious with her for getting pregnant when he hadn't given her permission to do so. She gave our baby brother that name because she had faith that he'd grow up to be a good man despite her mate, and live by his own set of rules. Or something along those lines."

Pest nodded. "I wanted her to name him Faith so I wasn't the only one stuck with a girly name. I got voted down."

Glacier winked at Creed. "Neb and I said no. You're welcome. Creed was the best name of the ones Mom considered. It's very masculine too."

"Dick," Pest muttered. "Where were you when I was born?"

"Learning how to fly and imagining all the ways I could torment you when you were older, Tempest."

Creed offered them knives, forks, and napkins. "Here. Don't stab each other."

Angel grinned. "I like your family."

Creed came to her side and wrapped his arm around her. "Don't say that. They might want to visit us often since we're stuck here for six months."

Pest nodded. "Next time make side dishes. A cake or pie would be sweet, too. Do you cook, Angel?"

"I do. My mom taught me."

"Finally, someone in this family can. I'm so coming over every time I come to the cliffs." Glacier winked.

"He does that a lot," Creed murmured. "We think something is wrong with his left eyelid with the way he twitches it so often. He thinks it's cute. That's why he's still single. Totally clueless."

Pest laughed. "That, and his eyes freak the fuck out of the Lycan packs. Tell them what they called you at the last guardian gig you did."

Glacier took another bite and growled low.

"I might be dubbed Pest but it beats the hell out of Ghost Eyes. He also got compared to a Siberian husky. Ever seen the ones with blue eyes? One Lycan asked if he was a shifter from that dog breed."

Angel fought a laugh. Creed didn't bother to hide his amusement and his body shook.

"I hate you," Glacier sighed. "Really. This is why none of us see each other often and ask to be sent on assignments away from the cliffs. Who needs enemies when I have brothers?"

"You love us," Pest taunted. "Deep, deep down you also enjoy being given shit."

"I want to thank you both for what you did by fighting at my side." Creed grew solemn. "You saved my life."

"Thank you," Angel added. "Creed means everything to me."

Her mate smiled down at her. "You mean everything to me too."

"Shit. They're going to get all mushy and make out. Eat faster," Pest urged his brother.

Glacier nodded. "We don't do mushy." He looked up at Creed then. "We always have your back, baby brother. We just don't have to hide it anymore with dickhead gone."

"We always knew he'd make it harder on you if we didn't." Pest paused. "You belonged to the clan, and that gave him the power to make your life miserable."

Angel watched the brothers tease each other and joke around for the next half hour before they left. Creed bolted the door and she went to him, wrapping her arms around his waist.

"I almost lost you."

"Never." He kissed the top of her head. "You're stuck with me for millennia."

Chapter Eighteen

Three weeks later

Angel got off the phone with her parents. They were happy for her and Creed but didn't like that they wouldn't see her for another five months. Her time at the cliffs wasn't boring though. Gali and Renna visited her a few times a week while Creed went flying with his scout friends. The time she spent with him made her happier than she'd ever been. She liked to think of it as their honeymoon.

The door opened and Creed walked into their bedroom. He'd spent a few hours with one of his friends in the training room. She sniffed. "You smell really good."

"I worked up quite a sweat fighting."

"You were fighting?"

"Sparring. Delbius thinks I've grown a bit rusty being a guardian. I proved him wrong. Let me take a shower and we'll have lunch together."

"I'll make us something."

"I'll hurry. I'm starving."

"Sandwiches then. They're fast." She headed toward the door.

"I love you, Angel."

She spun at his words and found him still standing in the same spot, watching her. Amusement sparked in his eyes. A slow smile spread on his lips.

"Did you just say what I thought you did?"

"I *love you*, Angel."

She rushed at him. He caught her and pulled her into his arms, lifting her off her feet. She wrapped her arms and legs around his body. He was sweaty but she didn't care. He'd said the three words she had wanted to hear the most, and he'd done it out of the blue.

"I. Love. You." He brushed his mouth over hers. "I finally figured out I've felt it for a long time, but today it hit me, what all these feelings inside mean."

"What happened today? I mean, well...you know what I mean."

"I ran into Lord Aveoth. He asked if I'd still like to be guardian to your pack once the five months are up, but he made it clear it's my choice. I'm part of the clan now, instead of in service to it."

"That's amazing!" She was thrilled. "What made him do that? I thought he was going to give you your freedom in ten years?"

"He made it an official law first thing this morning that no children are to be given in service to the clan. He freed me and the others who were sworn to duty when Lord Abotorus was the clan lord. It was as though a burden had been lifted from my shoulders, and it just hit me how much I love you. I have denied it for so long because I couldn't dare to dream of being with you."

"I love you too, and I've known how you feel. I've seen it in the way you look at me and when we touch. I'm glad to hear the actual words though."

"You've been so patient with me."

"I have been. I think you should reward me by carrying me into the shower with you and showing me how *much* you love me."

He turned with her in his arms. "You're just happy you don't have to train me to have great sex with you."

"I could pretend you're bad in bed though so we can spend a few days there."

"That sounds like a plan." He sat her on the bathroom counter and backed away. He reached up and tapped his jaw. "What's next? I forgot."

She laughed and slid off the edge, standing. "Get naked."

"Oh, that's right. Then we talk about the weather to get aroused. Sunny days turn me on. How about you, baby? Are you a sunshine person or dark clouds?"

She loved that he played with her now. "I'm into any weather that's around when you are." She began to strip off her clothes. "As long as we're not wearing clothes."

He turned on the water. "Hot rainstorm it is."

"I like it when you make me wet."

He laughed. "I've got us covered then."

She climbed into the stall first, since she had fewer things on than he had to remove, and held out her arms. "Hurry up."

"We have forever."

"We're still making up for time lost."

He stepped into the shower and pinned her against the wall. "In that case, I need to tell you how much I love you all the time."

Angel grinned. "I think I prefer you showing me. Stop talking and get to it."

He slid his hand into her hair and cupped her ass with his other hand, kissing her. "I can do that."